A Quiet
Ente

By

Peter Wynn Norris

 New Generation **Publishing**

To

Rachael

Peter Wynn Norris

ACKNOWLEDGEMENTS

Uganda is a beautiful country straddling the Equator. I went there as a green Police Inspector and I have many to thank for helping me to understand the country and its people. There are too many to acknowledge them all so I have picked those who still stand out in my mind.

An early influence was Station Sergeant Mulemezi. He was my unofficial mentor at Kampala Central Police Station. During the war he had served in the bloody campaigns in Ethiopia and I still recall conversations with him about the Kings African Rifles. Tom Ngirenta was a Police Sergeant whose dedication, inventiveness and wit became a yardstick for my expectations of other Uganda Policemen. I am certain Detective Sergeant Sitanule Oboran had no peer in his profession. Speaking at least eight languages his network for gathering information was vast. And then there was Paulo Odongto. He was my clerk but I learnt more about leadership – and the Acholi language - from him than from any other source.

I am sure none of them would recognise the strength of their contributions to my development. My regret is I didn't tell them; though in retrospect I probably didn't recognise it myself. Often I wonder what became of each of them in the turbulent times that bedevilled such a wonderful country.

My greatest thanks go to my wife, Pam, who somehow has tolerated me disappearing for long periods into my writing.

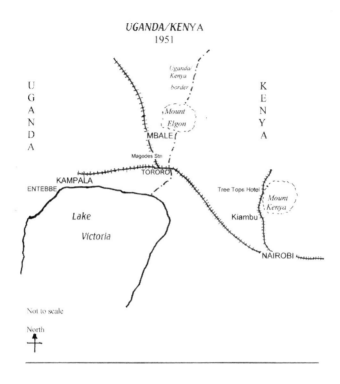

UGANDA/KENYA
1951

Uganda/Kenya border

U
G
A
N
D
A

K
E
N
Y
A

Mount Elgon

MBALE

Magodes Stn

KAMPALA

TORORO

ENTEBBE

Tree Tops Hotel

Mount Kenya

Lake

Victoria

Kiambu

NAIROBI

Not to scale

North

Approximate distances by road:
Entebbe/Kampala: 22 miles
Kampala/Mbale :180 miles
Mbale/Tororo: 38 miles
Mbale/Nairobi : 370 miles

Key:
Railway

AUTHOR'S NOTE

In the early 1950's – when this story is set - the East African territories of Uganda and Kenya were a loose form of confederation with Tanganyika having the common services of Posts and Telegraphs, Railways and Harbours and currency. However, the differences between the two countries were marked. Uganda was a Protectorate and Kenya a Crown Colony. Many of the Europeans in Kenya had been there for decades, some being second, third or fourth generation with a widespread belief among the "settlers" that the country would never gain independence. In sharp contrast none of the Europeans in Uganda were permanent residents, most being on Colonial Service or local contracts or with international trading companies. Missionaries were among the earliest of the Europeans to arrive. All were aware that independence would come; though most thought this would be later rather than sooner. In 1948 Kenya's total population was five and a half million of which five and a quarter million were Africans and the rest non-African (Asians, Arabs and Europeans). Uganda's total population was just under five million of which forty-one thousand were non-African. Of the non-Africans only six thousand were Europeans and they could not own land. By contrast, in Kenya vast tracts of the country were owned and farmed by Europeans – indeed, immediately after World War II the UK Government was still encouraging British people to take up farming in Kenya. The question of land tenure around Mount Kenya had been a powerful cause of resentment among African people and contributed to the insurrection that took place in the early 1950's. In both countries the Asian populations outnumbered Europeans.

Mount Elgon is an extinct volcano. To reach the highest parts requires few mountaineering skills, just stamina and the will to keep walking when the air becomes very thin. In Uganda its lower reaches supported world class Robusta coffee. At the time of this story many of the local population were skilled at growing this and with the help of the Government's Co-operative Department thriving businesses developed.

Entebbe Airport is in Uganda, a mile or so from the Township of Entebbe. In 1951 its runway was extended to give it international status, with aircraft taking off and landing over Lake Victoria, a vast ocean-like expanse of water. Entebbe was the Headquarters of the Protectorate Government.

PROLOGUE

Mbale Eastern Uganda 1948

Juba Wanyama was an exceptional student. No-one knew this better than Father Cornelius O'Hagan who had fought hard for his admittance to the College when the boy arrived, parentless and penniless. Now, four years on, the priest stood perspiring in the gymnasium, watching him sparring. Juba was the tall one with wide shoulders, well muscled for his eighteen years. Well, probably eighteen – who could be certain when births were not registered but just noted by the events of the time.

He moved cleanly, fast, reminding him so much of himself all those years ago. Con O'Hagan the Battling Mick they called him. Cruiser weight, Golden Gloves contender New Jersey USA. 1926, was it? Could – should – have gone further if it hadn't been for those Celtic emotions. Lack of self control had cost him the chance. The sounds from the ring cut into his day dream. 'Juba, stop fighting. Spar man, spar. Your defence needs sharpening.'

The youth took no notice. He continued to flail into his opponent, bloodying his face. In a way that denied his years the priest skipped through the ropes and stood between the boxers, parrying the last blow, unable to stop the rich blood dripping onto his white cassock. He took the towel from round his neck, wiped the blood from the victim's face and checked to see the injuries. Then he led the tall youth through the ropes to a wooden bench on the veranda.

'What was going on, Juba? Your defence is weak. That army sergeant will get through it even though he's all brawn. Don't you want to do well in the Championship? It's not long now.' Out of all the boys he had trained in his thirteen years at the college this one had talent. The will power, guts and a lot of cunning too. Not only that, he also had the physique. He had to admit to a nagging twinge of guilt. Was he hoping to relive his fighting days through the boy and feel the success he never achieved? The youth looked at his feet and breathed heavily through his mouth, his chest rising and falling. He held out his hands for the priest to remove the gloves.

'Well? I haven't got all evening.'

'I was angry.'

'What did he do to make you angry?'

'It wasn't him. It was my thoughts.'

'You're not making sense … '

'I will tell you what troubles me. Why are there so many Wazungu - white people – in our land? They have the good jobs and the money and good food and … that's what makes me angry.'

The priest cocked an eyebrow. 'Who put these ideas in your head?'

'No-one. They are my ideas. I burn inside.'

Cornelius Hagan, veteran of the Easter uprising at Dublin Post Office in 1916 when he was so young, knew what he wanted to say but what came out was, 'If you want to be Champion you have to beat that army sergeant. He depends on his muscles but you're faster and can counter punch and …'

'That is not what I want to talk about,' the youth shouted, 'I want you to tell me what I should do …'

'Do? About what?'

'About what I have just told you.'

'It's not for me to say, my son …'

'Yes it is. Or are you the same as all the other Wazungu?'

The young boxer had laid down the gauntlet; Con O'Hagan never ducked a challenge. 'All right, Juba. I will tell you something I have told to few other people. A long time ago, when I was about your age, an alien people were running our country. We did what we thought was right. We took up arms against them.'

'And what happened?'

'There was fighting. A lot of guns were fired. A lot of people died ....' *and are still dying; then I took off for America and now I'm here in Uganda, he thought. But he didn't say this.*

'So that is what I should do. Get lots of guns? And fight.'

'That's not what I meant. You can't ...'

'You give us education but we are dominated by your religion. An alien religion.' He mimicked the priest's way of talking. 'It's the same thing that you have just told me. If you could do that I must do what you did.'

'They're strong words, Juba. I think you had better get under the shower, cool down and we will talk about this later. Come back and see me in an hour. I will wait for you here.' Juba slung his towel over his shoulder and marched off in the direction of the dormitory.

Con O'Hagan settled himself on the verandah. He had papers to mark but he couldn't move his mind from the boxer. How well did he really know Juba? There was always some rebelliousness in the lad. Lad? A lad no longer. He had made his mark in the College in all sorts of ways. His physique, quick mind and boxing prowess gave him status but what did the other students think of him? Con O'Hagan realised he didn't know the answer to this. Only one person seemed to be close to him. James Olumu. He had often seen the two of them playing mweso –African chess – and on other occasions talking together, with Juba pounding his fist,

10

driving home a point. It reminded him of young men in the movement all that time ago.

The hour had gone and Juba had not returned. It was dusk as he saw his protégé's distant figure, a kitbag on his shoulder, hurrying along the jacaranda lined red earth road that led out of the college. Con O'Hagan felt guilty; he had lit a fuse and he had no idea what would blow up. This he did know, though. Juba would not return.

When he had come to the College those years ago he had pleaded for admission even though he had no money for fees or books. Con O'Hagan recognised his intelligence and he persuaded the principal to take him in. Now he had passed the highest level of examinations he could take at the College and if he had stayed and fought for and won the Uganda championship he would have been on his way to the Olympics. Was he going to waste all this in some ideological struggle?

You can talk, Con O'Hagan, he said to himself.

ONE

May 1951

Night on Mount Elgon has a stillness that charms. The air has a feel of velvet and is so thin that every sound slips through it. The rippling of the mountain streams, the wind through the groves of bamboo, the whispering of the maize leaves as they rustle together, night birds far away, and the sounds of people – particularly people. Juba Wanyama and his companion sat in the rocks high above the village. There was enough moonlight to see the houses, the animal pens, the granaries, thatched with reed.

In his compound on the edge of the village minor chief Yoweri his wife and his three children slept. It was that time of the night when people sleep their deepest. And yet Yoweri heard the sound. Human, not animal. So close. He slid from his bed, felt for his short spear in its place against the wall and moved as quietly as he could to the door. His house was of the traditional design. Round, no windows. He felt for the door latch string, crouched, ready to spring out, and tugged gently. There was no movement - the door was stuck. He pulled harder. It still wouldn't move. He heard the crackling, smelt the smoke. He pulled frantically. Desperately. The string broke and his hope of moving the solid hardwood door plummeted. Fanned by the gentlest of breezes the flames had spread from the dry outer surface of the thatched roof into the wet inner layers sending thick heavy smoke billowing into the living space. He took the fumes in by the lung-full. The ochre-coloured earth which had plastered the wooden framework began to drop in red hot chunks onto the firewood piled under the shelter of the overhanging roof. More dropped into the inside of the building where it fired whatever it touched. Yoweri was on his knees, spluttering, coughing, retching, choking. He was so overwhelmed he couldn't reach his family at the other end of the room. In the few minutes it took for them to perish the men he had heard were far from his compound.

By the time the first of the villagers reached the hut the fire had spread to the thatched granary and goat compound alongside the main building. The screams of the terrified creatures as they burned to death was more noise than the humans raised between them as they choked on the fumes. The villagers could only watch, powerless to do anything more.

Dawn's layer of mist held down the smoke and the smell of both the smouldering ruins and the charred bodies still lying inside. Every member of the village stood quietly in the compound, heads shaking, tongues clicking. Then a mournful dirge started and gradually it was picked up until everyone had taken it on their voice.

Cecil Woodley-Wills, the District Commissioner, made the short walk to the Police Station. He preferred to see people in their offices. He hated phones, a legacy of his early years in remote stations when he regarded phones as tools of the devil for conversations between bureaucrats in Entebbe and Kampala. He strode into the office of the District Police Commander. 'Hello, Tug. Got a minute? I'm sure you have,' and he planted his tall frame on the bench by the window. The District Police Commander, 'Tug' Wilson, eased his chair back, pointed to the papers on his desk and put his pen down. 'It's that well known work of fiction, the Quarterly Crime Return and that can wait.' The DC outranked the other officials on the station, but he affected a disarmingly vague manner. His track record was formidable; with first class honours from Oxford and a rowing Blue he was recruited into the Uganda Administration in 1927. The Head of the Civil Service had regularly wooed him to take a senior position in a Ministry but he had staunchly declined, choosing to remain in District Administration in remote areas. 'I'm staying where I know I can do something worthwhile,' was his response each time he was asked.

'Something's going on up the mountain. I've got a message from one of the chiefs. You'd better read it,' and he passed a sheaf of papers to the policeman.

Wilson spread the papers on his desk and read. After a while he looked up at the DC. 'So what have we got? A sudden death, probably a murder. No evidence to speak of and by the time we get there the scene will be cold. Still, what's new?'

'Go to the last page.'

Wilson looked again. 'You mean the mention of "dini" – that means religion in Swahili...'

'Cult is a better translation. Do you remember the Dini ya Masambwa?'

Wilson shook his head. 'Before my time. Heard the name, that's all'.

'In the thirties and forties it was strong in West Kenya, though it penetrated our side of the border. One of its aims was getting all Europeans out of the country. Nowadays the people on our side of Elgon have become so affluent I thought it had gone for good. We're a coffee grower's paradise. The growers aren't strong on organisation but the Co-operative Department has done their job sorting out their problems and promoting overseas sales. I don't think many would want to be without the Co-operative Officer.'

'What sort of trouble did Dini ya Masambwa

14

make?'

'In this District there was some rioting and a chief was killed, the claim being he was fair game since he was a servant of the British government.'

'So if Dini ya Masambwa hasn't been resurrected what is it likely to be?'

'That's what we've got to find out. I've heard the word "dini" has been going round lately and of course we have the death of the chief. If it is a new cult, it won't have gathered the same force. Yet.'

'I was talking to someone in the Kenya Police recently and he was telling me about an organisation emerging around Mount Kenya. I suppose we can't discount a connection even though it's a long way away. I'll find out what Special Branch knows. But first we've got this death to look into. I'll have to get up there as soon as possible.'

'I shall be coming too.'

Juba climbed until the track petered out. The air was thinner now and he could feel himself gulping for oxygen. Habitation then the forest and its lofty hardwoods were well behind him. He was coming to the moorland where the giant groundsels and lobelias stood like sentinels guarding the heights. This was far enough. He sat in the crevice of a rock which gave him shelter from the wind and from where he could look up and see the dying sun glinting on the jagged peak the people of the mountain called Wagagai.

He wanted time to think. He had left Father Con's religion long behind him. It was two years since he had walked out of the College. Yes, he would like to have been heavyweight champion of Uganda. But that was behind him too. To achieve all that he would have been dependent upon a Muzungu and he was not going to be dependent on anyone. But he couldn't get it out of his mind. The white priest had been a great boxer in America and a revolutionary in his own country.

That was what he wanted now. Revolutionaries. He had been drawn back to the mountain after so many years because people were talking about the "Dini". And what had he found? Leaderless people who talked a good tale as they sat round the fires late at night, who did little things which irritated the authorities but no more than that. If it was to amount to anything the "Dini" needed young people with fire in their bellies, like those in Kenya.

In those months after leaving the College he had forged references and a school leaving certificate. He had no difficulty in finding work as a trainee assistant in the laboratory of the Tororo cement factory, 40 miles away. The Muzungu chemist, a fat old man, had tried to seduce him so he killed him. It had been easy. The murder was never solved. He had been too clever for the Muzungu detective they had sent all the way from Kampala. And this was what the "Dini" had to become, bolder, ready to kill Wazungu. The authorities were not ready for tough, determined action. Months earlier, he had visited Kampala. Now he had got word that what he had arranged had been successful. James had not let him down. This was going to stir up these people. It would show them he was serious.

The sun had slipped away while he had been absorbed in his thoughts. He could no longer see Wagagai. There was no moon; it would be difficult finding his way back so he wrapped his cloak tightly round him and forced his back deeper into the rock. It was going to be cold but he would rather sleep there than face the descent.

TWO

Rosemary Woodley-Wills cherished her interlude of privacy from just before dawn until Cecil stirred an hour later. Each day she made her way to the hardwood steamer chair on the back veranda. There as the sun came up she could gaze upon Nkokonjeru, the dark sombre looking bluff which marked the start of the foothills of the mountain. Some times in the wet season she could just make out the streams tumbling from its heights. She delighted in the sunrises, never the same two days running, being pulled into the soft darkness, waiting for the first colouring of the sky.

She didn't want to think of the events for the coming day - the petty committee meetings and presentations – more of the same. She just wanted to ... to ... she couldn't gather her thoughts. Well what did she want? She knew. She had known for some time now. *To be herself.* She couldn't remember when she last felt she was her own person. She was the DC's wife with all that meant. If the Colonial Office had had their way she wouldn't even be that. Cecil had broken an unwritten code of practice. It was unacceptable for a young official, fresh from university, to marry before he had completed his first overseas tour of duty. As soon as the results of his course were announced Cecil had been appointed to the Colonial Service. Still in Oxford he had completed a training period and at the end of this he was confirmed in his appointment to the Administration in Uganda. They had married as soon as this was announced by which time is was too late for his appointment to be revoked.

Why had she married Cecil? Did she really know? Did love come in to it or was it that she had been flattered that a student at the University - and a member of the boat crew – wanted her. Whatever it was, it had not stopped her delighting in their earlier days in remote up-country stations where everything was so informal, accompanying her husband on his safaris into "The District". No motor transport then, just her feet and, if lucky, a bicycle. She had relished coping with the hard conditions, softened all the time by the humour and companionship of the African porters who carried their equipment. Now in a fast growing Township with a bigger population of both Europeans and Asians she felt on show and yet anonymous at the same time. Would it have been different if there had been children? There would have been other mothers; she had seen how relationships changed when families appeared. She would never experience this now.

'Snap out of it, Rosemary. You're getting maudlin. It's in your hands. It's your life. Do something.' She caught herself talking out loud; she did this too often these days. Cecil's fault? No, she couldn't blame him, though she did resent that he was the picture of fulfilment, always in control. Where would she be if they hadn't met? At least she should be grateful to Cecil. He had rescued her from an unpromising future. A farmer's only child on a remote patch of England. And a girl at that. Her father had always resented not having a son – and he let her know it. Constantly.

She must have dozed. She jumped as she felt the touch on her shoulder. It was now light. She turned to find her husband standing behind her, holding out a cup of tea. 'Time's getting on, Rosie.'

'Please Cecil don't call me that. You know I hate it …'

'That's a bit strong, isn't it? You seemed deep into your thoughts. Penny for them.'

'They're worth more than that. I don't know if I should sell them so cheaply.'

18

He pulled his chair close to her. 'Try me.'

After all the years they had been married could she really tell him what had just gone through her mind? She should stay on safer ground. 'I was thinking about you and the way we met.' He reddened, always uncomfortable when someone was talking about him. 'My friend Liz who worked in the library told me of this Adonis in the university boat crew. "A six footer with hair that waved like corn". So I cycled down to the river every morning, wrapped in a long scarf and heavy coat and rode along the tow path keeping pace as you skimmed along the Isis …'

'And I bet you thought I hadn't noticed you?' She nodded. 'You put me right off my stroke, those long legs pumping away.'

'So when you came into the library it wasn't – as you said - by chance.'

'No. I had done a little detective work.' He drank his tea. 'Well, that was worth more than a penny. How much buys me more?'

Rosemary felt her face colouring. 'I don't know if you can afford it, Cecil.'

'All very mysterious. If there was more time I'd see what's on offer. But I'm late. A chief has been murdered and it's got "big problems" written all over it. I've got to go with Tug Wilson up Elgon. I may be back tomorrow. Can't be sure. We'll talk about it then. OK?'

Cecil was gone. Rosemary sighed. 'You still don't understand, do you,' she cried out.

THREE

The DC drove his Chevrolet sedan into the police station compound followed by his safari truck loaded with all he needed for a short stay on Elgon. Strapped tightly on top of it all was his Raleigh Roadster bicycle. It was early and yet there was a reassuring bustle. Two constables were heaving camping equipment into a long wheel base Land Rover and he smiled as he recognised the cases of 'hard tack' rations buried under all the gear. Now he would be shamed into sharing the tinned delicacies that his own cook had packed. Uniformed policemen stood stiffly in a line while Tug Wilson carried out his briefing; then he closed his note book and turned to the DC. 'We're all ready to go. I thought we could make our first stop at the PWD road maker's camp. Scatty Muller has been up there for some time now. He might know something and even if he doesn't there'll be coffee on the go.'

The convoy started to climb Muller's new road which wound its way into the foothills. Looking like a giant inverted pudding basin Elgon straddles the border between Uganda and Kenya. Being spread over two hundred square miles disguises the fact that its main peak, Wagagai, is 14,000 feet above sea level. To the local people it was the sacred home of their time-honoured deity.

After two hours driving the road changed. Until now it had been newly laid murram and with heavy rolling the red earth had packed into a firm surface. From here onwards the old track was topped with rutted black soil, superb for cotton growing but slimy as a wet road surface. The noise of a diesel road grader skimming off the top earth signalled Muller's camp was near – a cluster of aluminium rondavels, sited by a fast running

20

stream and a compound for the road making machines and tools. The convoy pulled into the compound. The Road Supervisor, dressed in bush jacket, shorts and leather work boots that came halfway up his calves, was tending a wood fire over which hung a cast iron pot. 'You made it then. I've just got some coffee ready for you.'

The police superintendent climbed down from his Land Rover, straightening up and stretching to ease his aches. 'Smells good, Scatty. How did you know we were on our way? You've no phones or radio.'

Rubbing his blackened hands on a piece of cloth the South African walked over to the vehicles. 'I don't need those contraptions. I use the bush telegraph. I know all that's going on down in the Township. And often before it happens.' He poured steaming coffee into chipped enamel mugs and handed them to Woolly Bill and the police superintendent. 'The crockery's not much to look at but you'll forget it when you taste the coffee. Best in the world up here.' He motioned them towards a log alongside the fire. 'Bit chillier at this altitude. Hope you've got some woollies – no offence Cecil.'

'You know why we're here? Does your grapevine cover Elgon, too?'

'I suppose it's that poor bugger of a chief they roasted. It takes something like that to drag you up here Tug. You'd have just sent your minions otherwise. There's something going on for sure but I don't know what it is. My lads talk to the locals – particularly the ladies of course – but none of them has reported anything other than vague rumours. Problem is they don't speak the local language. Even with a sleeping dictionary it takes time to get up to speed.'

Woodley-Wills wasn't surprised at his reply. Outsiders weren't welcomed on Elgon and none of

21

Muller's road gang came from this area. 'There is talk of a new cult – secret society if you like. Have you heard anything about this?'

'No. Nothing, I'm sure I would have heard something if that sort of thing is happening.'

Tug Wilson had banked on Muller having picked up some useful information. It was going to be a tedious investigation. 'You'll need to stay pretty watchful.'

'Don't worry about me, Tug. The lads have clubs and spears. And I've got "Old Trusty", my Mannlicher.' He pointed to the long rifle chained to the framework of his pick-up truck. 'Before you ask, it is licensed. I use it to hunt game for the pot and keep the odd leopard and baboon off. But if it will ease your mind I'll put extra security on at night. And I've got Simba of course.' He nodded towards the tawny coloured Ridgeback dog lying in the back of his truck, head between paws, eyeing the newcomers from under heavy lids.

It was late evening when the police and the DC reached their destination. Ruts, minor landslips and the general poor quality of the track waiting to be transformed into a road made the going painfully slow. Making camp in the darkness was mercifully the last of the day's chores.

The following morning Wilson and his policemen went into the village to visit the scene of the fire and start enquiries. It was to prove a long and frustrating day for the police. They gleaned nothing from their investigations and the inspection of the chief's compound. If there had been any footprints they had been walked over time and again by the people from the village. There was nothing to show how the fire had started and by the time they had reached the scene the bodies of the chief and his family had been wrapped in bark cloth and buried. Interviewing the villagers yielded little. None of the police party spoke the local language and the Swahili of the villagers could express little more than superficial information.

The DC took his cycle along the rough tracks to see the Area Chief. He pedalled his way through puddles and ruts to the chief's office. A European on a bicycle was such a rarity that the local people ran alongside him, cheering and shouting "Bwana Baisekili". Chief Erinayo Kazinga was on the long veranda of a single storied building roofed with corrugated iron. In front standing in a circle of whitewashed stones was a flagpole flying the red, white and blue Union flag.

'I'm honoured by your visit, Effendi. I thought it would just be the police coming.'

'Ah, Erinayo. On the contrary, you honour me with the term Effendi. I think that's the old soldier in you coming out. I have to tell you that I have come because I am concerned for your people. What did you mean when you said there are rumours of 'dini'? The last thing I want to do is to send the army up here to search out such a thing. You've been in the army – KAR wasn't it - and you know what their coming would do to your area.'

'The army, yes it would be terrible, I know.' The Chief paused, appearing lost in thought. Then he said, 'There are always such tales. Maybe it is nothing. I'm not very good at making reports. My clerk writes them from what I tell him. I didn't say anything about a dini. Why should I?' He shrugged his shoulders. 'People don't talk to me about such things. I know nothing about how Yoweri was killed. There are some who say he didn't put his cooking fire out when he went to sleep. He was a good man. Stubborn, though. He would argue with people. Maybe that's what got him killed.' He continued ducking the DC's questions. There was no point in Woolly Bill pressing the chief any more.

23

They continued talking about administrative matters until Erinayo signalled the end of the discussion by calling for two gourds of sorghum beer. Together they drank, slowly sucking the sweet sour fluid using dried onion stems as drinking straws.

Thirty minutes later the DC remounted his cycle moving less steadily than when he arrived. He was well on his way to his camp when the screaming stopped his pedalling. There was a rumble of voices, more screams, the sound of branches being torn from trees. He dismounted. A woman was lying, writhing, in the middle of a mob. Men flailed at her with sticks and the women, waggling their fingers in their mouths, kept up an ululating scream. Blood oozed from wounds on her head and legs. A man swung a branch ripped from a mango tree at the woman but it never reached her. The DC had stepped through the crowd, catching the branch in mid-blow. Holding the crossbar of his cycle with one hand and the branch with the other he was an imposing figure to these villagers. 'You,' and he pointed to two women standing near the victim, 'help her to her feet. Someone get a chair and let her sit. Get water and clean her wounds. The rest of you, go and do something useful.'

As the crowd started to drift away he spotted one of the village elders. 'Yakobo, come and talk to me.' The old man pulled his goatskin cloak closer round his shoulders and looking sheepish walked slowly over to the DC.

'Why was she being beaten?' Silence. 'Come on, Yakobo. There must have been a reason. Has she stolen something?' Fatal thief beatings were all too commonplace though women were seldom targets.

'How do I explain what we know to a Muzungu?'

'Try me. Am I not speaking your language?'

'Eeh..eeh...eeh... even so you won't understand.

She has stolen souls of our people.'

'She is a witch, that's what you are saying? '

'Come, I will show you,' and he motioned for the DC to follow him to a house tucked away in a banana grove. The thatching of the granary had been torn off and there on planks of wood were fragments of brick clay. The DC could see that they were the remains of statuettes and miniature busts. 'People broke them into little pieces when it was discovered what she was doing.'

'Really, Yakobo, what is the harm in making these?'

With difficulty Yakobo lifted the wooden plank. Beneath it was a second plank and on it were seven figures, intact, beautifully sculpted in brick clay. Every personal feature was there. Facial and bodily adornments, scars; even strands of hair looked as though they would yield to touch. Each statuette had been polished until the skin shone black.

'Why, these are magnificent. I have rarely seen such sculpture. You are saying she made these?'

'Yes. They are such true images of people here. What other reason has she for making them than stealing peoples' souls?'

'What is her name?'

'She is called Flora. She is from Elgon. She has lived here for as long as anyone can remember. She had a husband once. He wasn't from here though. He went a long time ago. No-one knew she was capable of doing this. Some say she takes these little people and sells them to Wazungu. Why would she do that?'

The DC knew the woman would surely be killed if she remained here. He walked over to her. The blood had been wiped from her wounds. 'Old mother, if you stay here they will kill you, you know that.' She opened her eyes and nodded. 'I will take you back to Mbale with me until you decide what you want to do.'

FOUR

Rosemary turned the pages of her diary. What was her day going to be; worthy causes, all of which she could do without? The Town's Women's Guild meeting. Ten o'clock. And, yes, she was chairing it yet again.

The European Club where the meeting was to be held was a comfortable walking distance from her house. The sun hadn't yet heated the day as she strode along the jacaranda tree lined road to reach it. With the trees' flowers shed and lining the roadside like bluebells she could imagine she was walking in Oxfordshire. The club building was basic, no more than a large concrete block shed, thatched with reed, a bar at one end, now shuttered with an expanded metal grill. It served, also, as a pavilion for the cricket ground. The steward had put tables together and if the stale beer smell could be ignored the room was presentable enough for the meeting. At least, she thought, it was neutral ground.

The meeting took its predictable course. The state of the Township roads, rubbish and - ugh – sewage clearance, festivals to be held … she found her mind wandering. 'Mrs Woodley-Wills.' Mrs Patel, wife of the proprietor of the Mbale Gujarat General Stores was raising her voice. Had she dozed off? 'Please I have any other business.' Rosemary nodded for her to continue. 'We are hearing that there will be royal visitors in Kenya. Why are we being overlooked here in Uganda? We are so close to Kenya.'

'Mrs. Patel, these matters are all arranged in London.'

'But Mr. Woodley-Wills is an important man. He must plead for us. He is your husband. You must persuade him.' "Any other Business" dragged on and it was noon before Rosemary closed the meeting. By the time she had gathered her papers everyone had left except Mrs. Khan, the stationmaster's wife.

'It was a long meeting, Mrs. Woodley-Wills.'

Rosemary smiled. 'It often is. I don't know how to shorten it. And by the way, my name is Rosemary.

'Rosemary - I didn't know that. May I say something? You were not yourself today. I think that sometimes you were not with the meeting.'

'Did it show that much?'

'I was bored. I found myself watching you.'

'Well, sometimes I am bored too. I have to come but you don't have to, surely?'

'Apart from preparing food for my family and cooking and looking after the house what else have I to do? No one seems to want me to have other interests and this is the one thing my husband approves.'

'You didn't tell me your name.'

'It is Nasiha.'

'Nasiha, I think you and I have a lot in common then ... when I was twelve my teacher recommended me for a scholarship to a Grammar School. I was overjoyed. Then my father said that girls didn't need education.' Nasiha was nodding her understanding. 'Tell me, do you think of me in any way other than *Mrs. District Commissioner*? All I do is the little bits and pieces that my husband needs to be done but doesn't have time for.' She stopped abruptly. She felt the heat in her cheeks. What on earth was she doing, baring her soul like this?

The stationmaster's wife leant forward across the table. 'Naturally my marriage was arranged for me by my parents. I suppose that was so in your own case.'

Rosemary smiled at the thought. 'No, Nasiha, it's not our way ...'

'Oh, I didn't know that. I assumed this is the way it

always happens. I must apologise for not knowing.' The station master's wife blushed but she continued, 'Do you know, all of our names have meanings. Nasiha means "one who gives valuable advice." I am going to be true to my name. My advice is, do something you would never have thought of doing. Something you think you can't achieve, yet something that will change a person's life.'

'You should be a counsellor, Nasiha.'

'My parents were like yours. I wanted to study psychology but they wouldn't hear of it ... it wasn't a proper subject they said, not like accountancy or medicine. And girls don't need to study, of course.'

'That's a shame. You're cut out for it.'

There was a cough from the back of the room. Rosemary turned to see the club's African steward standing looking at them. 'Yozefu thinks we ought to go so he can shut up shop. I'm going to take your advice, Nasiha.'

Rosemary walked back to her house. She would just get there before Cecil came for lunch. And thinking of her husband took her back to what Nasiha had assumed – that her marriage had been arranged by her parents. Well, maybe in a contorted sort of way it had been. What made her make up her mind so quickly when Cecil proposed?

Flora was now installed in one of the servants' quarters at the rear of the Woodley-Wills house. Rosemary walked over to see her each morning but felt almost afraid of the woman. She couldn't speak – she knew Flora was mute, but she was still disconcerted by this. The only time she seemed to come to life was when Rosemary resorted to mime to ask to see the statuettes she had managed to bring with her when Cecil had saved her from the mob. Rosemary guessed she had no clay with which to continue her craft and she couldn't overcome the problem of her being unable to speak to find out about this. What had the Station Master's wife said? *"Do something you think you can't achieve, something to change a person's life."* Over coffee after dinner she summoned up the courage to tell her husband what she was going to do. 'I've come to a decision, Cecil. I'm going to take Flora under my wing.'

Woolly Bill raised an eyebrow and sipped his coffee. 'Flora? What on earth has given you that idea? You know nothing about her. Even the servants just shrug their shoulders when I ask them.'

'I know she's a mystery. There's the statuettes and the "stolen souls" and someone said she's a witch? But I don't care. You've introduced me to more fearsome witch doctors than her. I went over to her room this morning and looked at the statuettes. They're beautiful. I'm going to help her capitalise on her talent.'

'You're going to do what? You do realise that she can't speak?'

'I went to the College this afternoon to present prizes. I talked to Father Con. I told him she's a mute and it's impossible to communicate with her. He said that she has always lived on Elgon and if she's not deaf too she will understand the local language and he will teach me to speak it.'

'There's the first stumbling block, … I know O'Hagan is quite an expert on the local language but …'

Rosemary continued as though her husband hadn't spoken. 'Father Con is going to teach me enough to get through to her.'

'I just hope you know what you have let yourself in for. So let's suppose you can communicate with her' … did Rosemary hear scepticism in his voice … 'where does she get her clay? She's going to need a supply of that if you're going to help her continue her sculpting.'

'As it happens they have always made their own bricks at the College. You've often remarked on the lovely colour of the chapel and that's all brick. Fr Con knows a place on Elgon where there is a seam of fine quality brick clay. He's going to let me know where it is.' Her husband was about to speak but she continued, 'I tried to help her make an oven with charcoal and biscuit tins this morning but it didn't work and so I've seen the PWD foreman and he's going to make her a proper oven ...'

'Rosemary , you can't do that.'

'Yes I can ... and have. And don't worry I shall get them to cost it properly and I shall pay for it. What's the matter, Cecil, you're looking put out.'

'You might have let me know before you went ahead with all this.'

'Didn't you know, you were busy.' Rosemary smiled sweetly.

'You drive a man hard, Rosemary,' said Father Con. For a month they had been meeting early in the morning and again each evening until late. 'I think you have a remarkable gift for languages. This is more difficult than Swahili. With no dictionary and no text books you can now talk to me easily and I've been at it for sixteen years.'

'The test, Con, is whether I can get through to Flora. What if she can't understand the language?'

'Don't be a pessimist. Of course she will.' It was still early morning. 'Let's go and give it a try.'

'What, now?'

'Yes, now, no putting it off. Let's go.'

When they arrived at Flora's room the woman was grinding maize with a pestle and mortar. She wore the same passive expression which hadn't changed since she arrived from the mountain six weeks ago. She nodded to acknowledge their arrival. The priest pushed Rosemary forward. Tentatively she began to speak, using local greetings. Flora's face lit up and she started signing with her hands.

'You've cracked it, my girl,' laughed the priest, his Irish brogue thickening in excitement. 'She understands what you say. All you've got to do is broaden your vocabulary and work out what her signs mean.'

Rosemary was content. It all seemed to be coming together. The oven for firing Flora's sculptures worked perfectly. Father Con had produced a small amount of clay and Flora's work was better than ever. But despite this the African woman seemed upset. It took time for Rosemary to work out that she was unhappy taking all that she had to give without being able to give anything in return. If Flora was to retain a sense of dignity Rosemary had to find a way to over come this.

Situated in Mbale's main street flanked by Indian shops was the Church Missionary Society Bookshop. Rosemary's negotiating with the manager had obtained space in the window to display statuettes and busts. Flora's name was soon on everyone's lips. When Rosemary told her of the first sale – which realised seventy five shillings – she broke into a shuffling jig, waggling her forefinger in her mouth for the ululating cry of joy. She didn't seem perturbed that no sound emerged. Perhaps she heard it in her head Rosemary said to her husband over dinner that evening. Cecil had little to say.

FIVE

They sat round a fire warming themselves as the chill winds from high on Mount Elgon penetrated the clothes in which they were wrapped. The reflection of the flames danced on the leaves of the bamboo grove, well away from the villages where no-one would dare to intrude. The leading members of Dini ya Mungu Wetu turned their attention to the young man who had forced his way into the cult's inner circle. His natural aggression appealed to some of them; it frightened others and it was they who were now questioning the cult's future direction.

A man known as Mbuzi leant closer to the flames. 'We listened to you when you said kill Yoweri. We know he opposed us. It would be a signal to the authorities, you said. He was only a small chief and now Bwana Deesee and the polisi have come and gone and everything is the same. We meet and we talk and talk. The only good thing to happen was the Deesee took that witch Flora away. What do we do now?' He looked at Juba under lowered eyelids. This man, educated by the missionaries, was young and he was wearing a colobus monkey skin cloak. These should only be worn by elders. This youngster professed he wanted to go back to the traditional ways and yet he did a thing like this. Why would no-one else speak out against this upstart? They all seemed in awe of him. He, Mbuzi, certainly was not. He was a hunter, an important member of the community. If he could kill buffalo he could face this man.

Juba flipped the cloak back over his shoulders. 'You are right to question me, Mbuzi. I have said little of my plans. I too wanted to see the reaction to the chief's death but to tell you the truth I didn't expect very much. What did we do to make everyone know it was our work? Nothing. Trust me. Soon we shall have the power in our hands, and I mean power in our hands, power we can touch, to make the authorities fear us. When it happens everyone will join us'.

There was muttering of approval but Mbuzi wasn't satisfied. 'Anyone can talk of power. Power can mean lots of things. Tell us what this power is. And when are you going to give us this power.' Mbuzi crossed his arms over his chest and looked round for approval for his stand. A few were nodding and he took this as support.

'This is a secret until I am ready. Things leak out. You will know soon enough, Mzee.' He used the Swahili word for "old man" and it was clear to all that this was used in scorn. 'I have one more thing to say. There is a movement in Kenya that wants the same things as us. Like us they live round a mountain. There has been trouble ever since the missionaries tried to stop the circumcision of their women. The people had always done that. It was their custom. I hear they are well organised and we can learn from them. I intend to go there and find out what I can.'

'If you go there they are likely to kill you as a foreigner trying to find their secrets.'

'My father was of their people even though he came and lived on Elgon. Because of that I speak their language. That will be my entrance key.'

The Third Class Up Mail train from Kenya to Uganda whistled long and low as it passed over the Kenya/Uganda border. Juba had achieved more than he expected from his visit to Kenya. Now he had something to tell them and he would make that old goat, Mbuzi, suffer for his scepticism. The Dini ya Mungu Wetu could not fail to grow and he would lead it. There was a hissing from the pneumatic couplings and the slightest screech of metal on metal as the brakes came into play, easing the train to a halt at Tororo Junction's long platform. Passengers, beggars with faces disfigured by syphilis or worse, pickpockets and others who had just come to experience the delight of being in the crowd all crushed noisily together.

He picked up his kitbag and squeezed his way out of the crowded carriage. He prided himself that his journey from Nairobi had cost him nothing. The Asian Travelling Ticket Inspectors for each of the stages had taken one look at this man who radiated belligerence and who made no move to purchase a ticket and decided one fare less was of little consequence. The Ticket Inspector for the last stage was on the platform talking to another Asian from the Railway. Now with help available would he demand the fare? Juba deliberately pushed close to him. The Asian averted his eyes.

He continued until he was in the throng around the tea stall. They told him at Kiambu in Kenya that the tea stalls at most of the stations were run by their people, an effective chain of communication. Now was the time to check that he could connect with the system. He watched as a tall African cut thick slices of bread and brewed tea. Juba shouldered his way closer. He hesitated and then he spoke in his father's tongue. 'It is cold at night on the train.' Neither the tea stall man nor any one else appeared to notice. It must be the language, he thought. And if they didn't understand it they were not of the movement. The man carried on cutting the bread without looking up. Juba was about to turn away when the man said, 'Only a fool travels without a thick coat.' Juba smiled; he was now in contact with the organisation. Still without looking up the tea stall proprietor pushed a mug of strong sweet tea

34

and a thick slice of maize bread towards him. 'That will warm you.'

It has worked. He could count himself as one of them. With the longest part of the journey behind him he only had to reach Mbale. He was almost back. The next stage was by train on the branch line and that left in three hours time. That night he would shake up the inner circle of the "Dini" with what he had learned about the organisation in Kenya, what they were capable of.

The station was nearly deserted except for the Railway staff now that the mail train had gone and there was no where on the station to make himself comfortable. He climbed the steps leading out of the station and made his way to a nearby thicket of mango trees. He felt tired. It was true; it was cold on the train especially when it crawled through the Kenya Highlands. He stretched out on the ground, his back against a tree, where the afternoon sun could warm him. Three hours to wait. He dozed.

The knife that pierced his skin over his ribs drew blood and brought him fast to his senses. A man he had seen waiting at the tea stall was crouching holding the knife but the voice came from his other side. Beside him lounged the tea stall proprietor. 'You seem to know who we are but who are you?' asked the man. The knife point jabbed deeper. 'I am Juba, from Elgon, I ...' The man cut him short. 'How do we know you're not a police spy? There are many who don't like what we are doing. And there are many who like the money they can get from the police. Why should you not be one of those?'

Juba found himself stammering. He was scared. No... no he wasn't. He had never been frightened of anyone or anything. 'I gave you the right words didn't I?'

'They were nearly right. Who taught you how to say them? Even though you speak in our language you have a strange accent. If you want to live you had better convince me.'

Juba felt his anger rising. Why did the fool not accept him? He told them of the Dini ya Mungu Wetu, of his father and of his visit to Kenya and of the people he had met there. He had names. He no longer felt the knife point.

'I know the people you have talked to. What did they tell you other than about the railway tea stalls?

'They said they liked the sound of what we have started on Elgon. The time will come when we can join forces. They want us to remain ready; there might be something we can do.'

The tea stall man nodded. 'I will check. If they don't vouch for you we will find you.' The two men rose and went off in the direction of the Township.

Juba caught the train to Mbale and by dusk he was in an over-crowded Peugeot 504 taxi bumping its way up the mountain road.

As is the way throughout Africa news of Juba's return spread quickly. The inner core of the Dini called a meeting near the waterfall on the Sipi River. The sound of the water hitting water after its fall of over two hundred feet made overhearing their conversation impossible. Juba, in his colobus cloak, stood as he delivered what he had learned. He did what he always did as he talked. He walked slowly round behind each of the ten men forcing them to crane their necks to follow him. 'They say what they are doing in Kenya is fighting a war. In a war you have to be ruthless and that is what they are. Are we not about to fight a war?' He watched as most of the heads nodded. 'They started small in number but they had to get people do things that help their cause. Do you know what they did?' Faces were blank. 'They make them take oaths.' Mbuzi sat shaking his head. 'What is wrong, Mzee? Do you know more than I do even though you haven't been there?'

Mbuzi looked up at Juba. 'They make people do terrible things as they take the oaths. I have heard this from some who have fled from their homes to Uganda to get away from this. They force them do things that are forbidden – that have always been forbidden - within their tribe. Is this what you want us to do here? Eeeeeee ......' Mbuzi continued shaking his head.

'We need all our people joining us. If the only way is to do as they do, so be it. I told you this is the start of a war. Do you not want the Wazungu to leave our country? Do you want the missionaries to stop telling us what gods we can worship?'

Mbuzi stood up. 'Of course I want these things but I cannot agree with what they are doing in Kenya. Our gods will take vengeance on us if we do. He faced the circle of men. He pointed his stick at Juba. 'If you listen to this man he will destroy us.' He pulled his cloak tighter to him and walked away.

Juba sat down. 'We don't need his kind. We need people who are strong in mind and in body. Where I have been they have a proper plan. True, they have oathing ceremonies. There is good reason for this. When they have taken the oath people don't inform against the organisation. If we do the same here it will make them support our "Dini". Of course, in Kenya they are doing much more. They are making the Wazungu who farm there frightened. They attack their cattle, they burn their crops, they poison waterholes, and they kill Wazungu. And the ones they pick to kill are those who think they are good employers. Then the other Wazungu will think "If these are the people who are killed what hope is there for the rest of us". And they will pack their things and take their families back where they came from.' He looked round the circle. Most were nodding. He had won the day. Now he had to back this up with more than words.

'This is what we shall do next …'

SIX

Mbuzi muttered to himself as he plodded along the track. He was still a hunter even though he was getting on in years and should be taking it easy, acting as a mentor to the young as was expected of older people. But he had been a hunter for as long as he could remember and he would continue to do so, even until he died. Hadn't he been taught by his father and by his grand father too? True, the variety of game on Elgon had diminished as the population grew but there was still sufficient for his livelihood if, like him, you knew where to look for it. And of course, if you had the knowledge and the skill to track and kill. All this coursed through his head as he made his way along the same track he had trodden for years. It became narrower here, more overgrown but there were signs of duiker and other small antelope. What he would really like today were some fine fat guinea fowl. They were becoming scarce but he had heard their familiar screech. In the past he had hunted in the traditional way with snares, bow and arrow and spear but as a concession to his dwindling powers he now sported a shotgun. He had traded his last major kill – a fat impala - for it.

The canopy of the forest was denser. Here and there were thick branches sweeping low making the track more like a tunnel. Mbuzi was still angry at what had happened at the "Dini" meeting. With all his experience wasn't he a man to be respected by his people, so why hadn't he been supported when he confronted the mission taught boy? He stumbled. The drop spear caught him at the top of his spine. The pear shaped twenty pound mass of stone and clay moulded around a razor sharp spear head was a traditional way of killing the bigger game such as buffalo, or more likely, ripping away flesh and leaving the animal grievously injured. Mounted on a branch over a track used by game it was triggered by a strip of vine across the path being broken. Mbuzi was so absorbed in his anger that he didn't notice it. Primitive as it was, it found its mark and Mbuzi was destined never to find his guinea fowl. He was still clutching the old Spanish shotgun.

When the "Dini" met that night Mbuzi wasn't mentioned but everyone present knew why he had died. The message quickly spread throughout the area. The local chief's policemen – totally untrained – asked a few questions and then reported that Mbuzi had been the victim of an unfortunate accident. It was illegal under Protectorate laws to use drop spears but who took notice of this? A report was written by the chief and sent by hand to the Uganda Police District HQ at Mbale. It was received four days after Mbuzi's death. A file was opened by a sub inspector and was promptly closed by the Crime Branch officer - "Accidental Death – No Further Action".

SEVEN

Eight o'clock in the morning and the DC's office was already sticky with the humidity of the gathering wet season. The more Woolly Bill had considered the security situation on Elgon the more he was unsure what the other Heads of Departments knew about it. One thing he held dear was the maintenance of Pax Britannica. Independence is assured he said to himself, and when it comes I want my District to be in as good a shape as possible.

It troubled him how little he knew about his fellow government officers' knowledge of what was happening on Elgon. He wanted no loose ends. The grapevine worked well and it could be guaranteed not only to spread the usual gossip about the District's personalities – often before events happened – but he didn't know if the weightier matters affecting work always did the rounds. With this new "Dini" he had to be sure they all knew as much as he did. He had called a meeting of the heads of the government departments for the District – Medical, Public Works, Veterinary, Forestry, Game, Agriculture and Police. The last to arrive was Charles Harkness, the Public Works Department manager. 'What's all this about Cecil? Meetings? You'll have an agenda and minutes next.'

'I don't think we'll ever get to that, Charles. Anyway let's get started. It's not often that we all get together other than at the club but there are a few things I think we need to talk about.' He paused. 'There is a new faction on Elgon. They call themselves Dini ya Mungu Wetu and if your Swahili is rusty that means "The Religion of Our Own God". I think Tug should tell us what he knows about this.'

The policeman looked at the pad in front of him.

41

'This is a new secret society, not the Dini ya Masambwa resurrected. I think it is significant that they have used Swahili for the title, not a local language, as if to announce their presence to everyone. I have no doubt they were responsible for the death of a chief but we have no hard evidence People aren't talking much. So far it seems to be confined to the lower slopes of Elgon but my real worry is they might be trying to tie in with what is happening in Kenya. Though our neighbours there are playing it down the word is something big is blowing up around Mount Kenya. Already it's very nasty and if on Elgon they copy what is happening in Kenya – or worse, join forces - normal people will be too afraid to give information. We know that someone from Elgon has been to Kenya recently. We don't know who it is and if he has returned yet. I am working on finding out how big the movement is and at what rate it is growing. If anyone picks up anything, however small, I need to know.'

Harkness leant back in his chair. 'Don't let's talk it up, Tug. When I first came out to East Africa in the twenties they used to say if there were only two of that Kenyan tribe left in the world there would be three secret societies. You're too used to chasing people like the Stern Gang around Palestine.' The policeman sighed at the reference to his Palestine Police background and what it implied. 'Look,' continued Harkness, 'I saw Muller who's making the road up there when he came in to collect pay and rations last month. He never mentioned anything and I gather the morale of his men is sky high. Surely if there is something going on he would know. He would have said something…'

Woolly Bill cut in. 'Thank you, Charles. All I can urge is that this is no time for complacency. If, as Tug says, this "Dini" should join up with what is happening around Mount Kenya the economy here will be blown to pieces. A lot of people depend on the coffee for a living and this is not just on the mountain. Everyone in the District will suffer. Matt Cunningham, The District Medical Officer caught his eye. 'You've got something for us, Matt?' The Medical Officer had a knack of putting his finger on matters that turned out to be significant.

Cunningham nodded. 'I've got something from the WHO. A particularly virulent virus has come to light at a Mission Hospital near Bumba in the Belgian Congo...'

Harkness interrupted. 'That's hundreds of miles away. How is that relevant to us?'

'Well, I'm not sure that it has immediate relevance but what the WHO has to say is worrying. This virus creates a haemorrhagic fever and its symptoms are nasty. Its incubation time can be as short as two days. Then sore throat, dry hacking cough, weakness, headaches, and lots of other horrible things – I won't bore you with them now. Death can occur within two weeks of contracting it ...'

The Forestry Officer broke in, 'Does the WHO have anything to say about how people catch this fever?'

The Medical Officer looked at the WHO briefing document. 'They are not sure yet but they believe it comes from bat droppings.'

Harkness shuddered. 'We've got a million of those bloody things circling over here every night.'

'Yes, but as far as we know none of them is infected. There's more ...'

'There always is.'

'The disease can also be spread by contact with an infected person's body fluids – blood and where pustules break open obviously, but I suppose also saliva and even sweat and urine. Charles was quite right. The

43

outbreak is several hundred miles away but it has killed some 400 people. And the real punch line is there is no known cure. So, I need any news of strange diseases as soon as you hear.' Matt Cunningham closed his file. There was a spontaneous burst of conversation.

Woodley-Wills coughed. 'Let's move on. I've got one more item. I've been speaking to the Chief Secretary in Entebbe. He told me that there is very grave concern about the King's health. He has never been very robust and he has recently had a lung removed.'

The Medical Officer knocked out his pipe into an ashtray. 'To be expected, he smoked like a trooper, they say.'

'Are you going to give up that damned pipe then,' chipped in Harkness.

The DC continued. 'They thought he was improving but now he's in decline. And this is where it comes closer to home for us. His Majesty put off the Royal Tour to Australasia last year but the Duke and Duchess of Edinburgh will take it on shortly. And while it's not for publication yet the Chief Secretary says they will be staying for a short time in Kenya on their way to Australia.'

'At a time like this with all the unrest there.' Tug Wilson shook his head. 'I'm glad I'm not in the Kenya Police.'

'Has this any practical implications for us?' asked the Veterinary Officer.

Woolly Bill shook his head. 'At this stage the Chief Secretary doesn't know. We're obviously closest to the Kenya border so if help in any form is called for it might have to come from here. But don't ask me what that might be. My crystal ball's on the blink.'

EIGHT

Scatty Muller woke early. He stood in front of his rondavel and surveyed the plain thousands of feet below him as he cleaned his teeth. Ever since he secured his job with the Public Works Department he had started his day soaking in the countryside around him. Africa shouldn't be about cities and gold mines and all the other trappings of "civilisation" that had been brought to the continent. Still, what more could he wish; working in the bush, no more visits to a Township than were necessary and a job where there were results anyone could see and measure. Road making was a life he enjoyed.

The row with his father, a farmer in the Transvaal in South Africa, had been brutal. Scatty could no longer accommodate the way the old man treated the Africans who worked for him and had remonstrated with him. A dyed in the wool Afrikaner, the old man had lashed out at him with his sjambok – the buffalo hide whip that always dangled from his wrist. That was the moment Scatty decided to pack up and go. He ended his relationship with his father and South Africa. He packed his Ford pick up truck with his few belongings and with his ridgeback dog, Simba, headed north without knowing what he was going to do.

He drove through the Rhodesias and Tanganyika until he arrived in Uganda. There he discovered something he had never thought possible in Africa, a country where black, white and brown seemed able to mix and work together without rancour.

He spat out, put his toothbrush away and poked the overnight fire into life. He swung the billy can of water over the heat and waited to make his first mug of tea. Soon the gangers would be up and getting ready for the day. And it would be a good day, too; it was the last day of the month, pay day. Once he had seen the work under way he would drive the fifty miles to Mbale and collect the money for his work force from the Accountant General's branch office. Then he would go out to the plain and hunt for some meat for the night's braai. To celebrate pay day he always provided his gang with a huge barbecue. In some places it had been hard to get the game and he had to buy goats but here there was no difficulty.

Now he was ready. He checked his rifle, took a packet of cartridges from the strong box and called his Headman, Petero Odoi, who came with him with on these hunting trips. 'What shall we look for today?' he asked as they drove away from Mbale.

'Whatever you please, Bwana Scatty. Wart hog might be good. Nice fat on them. Impala's nice meat. It all depends on what we find, I guess.'

They drove along a narrow track until they saw their first animals, a herd of Thompson's Gazelle. 'There's not much else. Tommy it will have to be.' Scatty reached for the Mannlicher and quietly eased the bolt to load. His first shot brought down a fully grown male. The headman nodded his approval as they reached the carcase. Together they swung the animal into the back of the truck and started the journey back to the camp on the mountain. They arrived as the road gangs were returning to the camp. Once he had paid their wages there was no need for Scatty to give instructions. The gazelle was hauled from the truck and was prepared for the spit.

Scatty towelled after he had been under his improvised shower – an oil drum hanging from a tripod - and dressed ready for the evening's feast and entertainment. With money in the gangers' pockets there would be beer and for some there would be something stronger. He wore his long sleeved bush jacket to keep the mosquitoes off his arms though he never wore anything other than shorts to cover his legs.

He gave Simba some of the meat he had taken from the gazelle, left the dog in the rondavel and walked the hundred yards to the braai. He insisted that the cooking was carried out at a safe distance from the equipment and fuel store. The smell of roasting meat roused his hunger.

The gazelle was large and there was more than enough meat for Scatty and all twenty two of his gang members. The beer - locally brewed from bananas and contained in large gourds - had been brought in and the drumming, singing and dancing were as good as ever as the evening turned into night and turned into early morning. Scatty sat on his bamboo chair and watched, beating time to the singing with his tin mug. All of his men came from the Tororo area. It was only seventy miles from their camp on the mountain but it might as well have been five hundred. Their language, their customs, their dancing was so different to anything to be found here.

He had been so absorbed that he didn't notice Odoi come and sit on a log beside him. He felt the touch on his shoulder. 'I didn't know you were there Petero. Good braai, eh?' They spoke in Swahili.

'It always is, Bwana Scatty. Good meat. You shoot well.' The African had lowered his voice.

'What's the matter, Petero? There's something on your mind.'

'I have heard something. … Maybe it's nothing. … I shouldn't worry you with it.'

'Let's hear it then I can judge for myself.'

'I have a local woman. She says there is going to be trouble. There are some who do not want the new road to be built. They say the Gavamenti is invading their area. She thinks they might do something about it but she doesn't know what … '

Scatty remembered what Tug Wilson had said when the chief was killed. 'We will have to put more guards on. We can't afford any damage to our equipment.' Recognising what the evening's entertainment had done to his men he added, 'starting tomorrow night.' The singing and drumming were dying down and gradually the last of the gangers were disappearing to their beds. It was late. He had no idea of the time since he had left his watch in the rondavel when he showered. He should turn in too. Instead he went to his truck and unchained the Mannlicher. He still had the box of cartridges in the pocket of his bush jacket. He picked up his torch and fixed it along the underside of the rifle's barrel.

The moon was riding the sky, reflecting off the mist that hung under the trees. He heard the baleful cry of a hyena. Probably smelled the remnants of the braai, he thought. There it was again. It was nearer now. Scatty had been around game all his life; the sound was not natural as though someone was imitating a hyena. The sound sharpened his senses. There were other noises and he couldn't recognize any of them. 'What the hell is going on?' he said out loud.

He crossed the compound slowly, keeping in the shadows until he reached his rondavel. Where was the welcoming growl from Simba? As he opened the door his torch picked out a pool of blood. In the middle of it was the dog's head. It had been slashed from its body. The rest of his companion was hanging from the light hook in the ceiling.

Scatty's anger boiled. He would go out and shoot, shoot, shoot. The words swilling around in his head sounded just like his father talking. 'Calm down Scatty and think. What good would that do you?'he asked himself. Simba had been his friend and guardian for years. Now his last link with South Africa had really gone. For a moment his head hung as the tears blurred his eyes. He wiped his eyes with the back of his hand, straightened up and dashed the fifty yards from his hut to the one Petero Odoi shared with five of the other gangers. There was no-one there. He went from hut to hut and each was empty. He ran to the vehicle compound where his truck was parked. He could smell the petrol before he reached it. The earth beneath the vehicle was sodden. Someone had holed the tank. He shone his torch on the stored barrels of petrol and diesel; all had been punctured.

A voice cut the stillness of the night. In English it said, 'First the dog, now we will kill you. Your African men don't love you. They have all deserted you, Muzungu.' He could hear people moving in the bush. To stay would be folly. If they would kill one of their own – that poor roasted bloody chief - they would certainly not hesitate to kill him. He had to get away. He knew the tracks for miles around the compound and his impulse was to run but he set off slowly keeping to the shadows and making no noise. The moon gave just enough light so that he didn't have to use the torch but still he slipped from bush to bush as he tried to keep to the narrow game track. Each time he stopped he could hear movement.

'Muz...ung...uuuuuuuuuuuuuu.' The voice, far behind him it seemed, cried again, an undulating wail. He stopped. Although a cold air swept down the mountain his shirt was sodden with sweat.

Stand and face whoever it was. Why not? He had his Mannlicher and he doubted if they would have firearms. 'Muzungu, you can run, you can crawl on your belly, but we will find you.' It hit him; although his bush craft in the day time was unquestionable he couldn't match Africans at night on their home ground. What they had done at his camp was serious and now with this disembodied voice calling to him their intentions were clear. They had scared off all his staff; they were after him and he was on his own.

He knew he should get away quietly but he couldn't stop himself from running. All the tracks he had used were going down the mountainside. He remembered too late that there was a small escarpment in this area. His feet went from under him and he was falling, slipping, small thorn bushes ripping his bush jacket and shorts. And still he fell. Cannoning into a rock he felt it cut deeply into his thigh. It seemed an age before his fall came to an end on a flat area. He remained still lying on his back, the pain in his leg shooting all the way up his body. He shut his eyes, trying to close out the pain.

When he opened them again it was light. Dawn was breaking. The braai must have gone on longer than he thought. Why wasn't he sitting on his bamboo chair? The fire was out. None of his staff was there. He was surrounded in mist. Where was he? He pulled himself to a tree and sat leaning against it. Behind him was the rocky wall of the escarpment and in front of him were trees. And there twenty yards away was his rifle, the torch still attached. Vividly it came back to him. The voice, the flight, the fall. Simba, poor bloody Simba. One of the few creatures in his life he had ever loved.

He started to crawl for the gun when he heard the voices, distant but carrying clearly. He reached it. The scope was still intact. He peered through it and scanned the side of the escarpment. There they were, five or six, coming slowly down a track about a mile away. They must be still following him. He had to find somewhere to hide. But where? He turned and searched the escarpment wall with his eyes. To his left through the mist he could just make out a dark area. It looked like the entrance to a cave. At least it would be cover when they found his tracks, as they certainly would. He crawled along the ground until he could see the opening, about thirty feet across. It foretold of a cave going deep into the mountain.

As he reached the entrance animal smells hit him. On one side the earth was pounded flat. Rock hard. On the other side the soil was muddy. The hyena tracks were fresh. With his leg caked in blood he knew that these scavengers would quickly turn predator when they realised he was alone and helpless. The jaws of a hyena could sever his leg with one bite. What was the alternative? To wait until the raiders were upon him or continue into the cave. He moved into its mouth. From there he would be able to see anyone approaching and could duck further into the darkness where he stood more chance of picking them off one by one. With the last remnants of his strength he crawled deeper into the unknown.

He didn't hear the elephants arrive. For such big beasts they were remarkably quiet. The first he saw was a huge bull silhouetted in the entrance. The animal raised his trunk in the air, testing the odours. And then the rest came in single file, treading lightly along the track beaten into concrete hardness by years of pounding by their feet. Scatty had heard tales from African hunters about elephants going into a particular cave on Mount Elgon for the salt in its walls but he had dismissed these as fanciful. Who ever heard of elephants going into a dark cave when their normal habitat was the greenery of the forest? He flattened himself against the wall. He would be trampled to pulp by these beasts. His fingers found a crevice. Repelled by the damp slime that lined the hole he knew there was no alternative to squeezing himself into the small space. He crouched praying the elephants wouldn't find him, hoping the foul smell would mask his own scent. The herd trooped deeper into the cave. He had no idea how many there were or how long it was before he heard the scraping noises from the blackness of the interior. With nothing else to do but wait and hope he became aware of his leg. The pain spread throughout his body. He could no longer think.

The sound of the elephants returning brought him to his senses. They came so close to his side of the cave that he could hear the rumbling of their stomachs. And then they were gone. He crawled out of the crevice. He found his torch still worked and when he shone it up to the domed roof of the cave he saw the bats. They covered every inch of the roof. And the slime now coating his legs and covering his wound was the slurry created by their droppings mixed with water that had seeped through the walls of the cave.

By the time he reached the mouth he was in no state to realise that he had been out of action for much of the day. He felt sick. He retched and nothing came up. He was short of breath. He was too weak to handle "Old Trusty". Leaving the rifle by the cave's mouth he crawled away towards some acacia trees, unobserved now since his pursuers – if that's what they were - had given up the chase.

He was no longer aware of anything.

NINE

At dawn that morning Manassi and his wife had set out from their village on the edge of the escarpment to collect wild honey from the forest. They followed the track they had used for as long as they could remember. It took them directly to the forest but there was always the prospect of elephants emerging to find their way into the cave and so they kept clear of the well trodden track. Their expedition had been successful. They had honey to eat and honey to sell and barter. Since they had heard nothing of the big beasts they took the track that passed in front of the cave to return home.

Manassi's wife was the first to see Scatty. She said nothing but nudged her husband, their usual warning that there might be danger. He walked cautiously towards the figure by the acacia tree. 'It is the Muzungu who makes the new road.'

'What is he doing here?'

'How would I know, woman.' He called out, 'Muzungu.' There was no movement. They made their way closer, listening in case the elephants came. Manassi prodded him in the ribs with his stick but there was still no movement other than the slightest rise and fall of his chest. He leant over Scatty and sniffed. 'He's still alive, but not for much longer. It must be the sickness.'

'What should we do?'

'Nothing. You heard me, it is the sickness. Don't touch him. The Dini were hunting him. We don't want them after us.' He picked up the sack holding the kerosene tins in which they had packed the honey.

'But he will die. I hear he is a good man. He shouldn't die like this.'

'With the sickness he will die any way. He must

53

have been in the cave. Anyone who goes in that cave dies. It is the way of things.' Manassi strode towards the track that would take them back up the escarpment, looking around to check no-one had seen them with the white man. 'Maybe,' he thought, 'I can make a little profit from this.'

Manassi finally made his mind up. Against his wife's wishes he sought out Juba. 'You were looking for the Muzungu road maker.' Juba remained silent. 'I know where he is.' Juba still said nothing. 'Isn't this worth something?'

Juba spoke at last. 'It's worth your life.' Manassi remembered Mbuzi and the drop spear. He swallowed hard. His continued existence was reward enough. 'Where is he?'

'He is at the mouth of the cave where the elephants go.'

'I don't know that place. You will take me there.'

Juba bent over Muller. He could see the man's eyes were closed. The blackened bruising on his forehead and a deep wound on his right thigh, now crusted with blood. The grime from the cave darkened his face and clung to what was left of his clothing. His leg was swollen and red.

'Is he still alive, Bwana Juba?'

'Why do you want to know?'

'There is a curse on that cave.'

'He's still alive. What do you know about the curse?'

'A long time ago hunters used to go in there but they became ill and within a few days they were too weak to talk, their skin burst and water came out. They died and so did some of the people who tried to help them. Although that was a very long time ago we have not forgotten it and no-one goes in there now. Will the curse affect a Muzungu, Bwana Juba?'

'Why shouldn't it, old man; they are only flesh and blood like us.'

Manassi's talk of the illness stirred thoughts in Juba's mind. The illness contracted by the hunters was embedded in the local lore. While at the College one of the Fathers had told him of a lethal plague on Elgon. It sounded much the same as the illness described by the honey collector. And, what was so interesting to Juba was the priest emphasised there was no known treatment for it. Here was a gift placed in front of him. All he had to do was work out how to use it. 'Manassi, go and find at least four of the men who worked on the road for this Muzungu.'

'But everyone knows they ran away from the road camp.'

'They are hiding. Some are with the women from our villages. You're a man of Elgon and a hunter. Find them. Get them. Bring them here. Get Mbuzi's ghost to guide you.' Manassi had no doubt about what Juba meant. He disappeared along the bush trail. Chance was guiding Juba's hands. The next piece of news to reach him triggered a plan in his mind.

Rosemary was at a loose end. Cecil had been summoned to Entebbe to meet the new Governor. He had left by car before dawn that morning with Matt Cunningham who also had business in Entebbe. For once she had no meetings, prize givings or other function dropped on her by her husband. Flora seemed to have become self sufficient. She wandered over to where the African woman was sitting outside her quarters. Conversation with the old woman – if it could be called that - was still a drawn out affair but at last Rosemary discovered she had no clay. Father Con had told her of the deposit of clay where he extracted all that he required for brick making for the College. It was forty or so miles into the lower reaches of the mountain, but Scatty's Road, as everyone now knew it, would take her close. It was a lovely morning. It would be even lovelier on Elgon. As well as four buckets and a jembe – an implement like an army entrenching tool which she had borrowed from her gardener - she packed a flask of coffee and some sandwiches and looked forward to picnicking at one of the spots where she could see out over the plains.

Yes, I know, she said to herself, Cecil would have been muttering that I shouldn't go, too risky, but Heavens alive he knows we've lived in wilder parts of Uganda than this. And she set off in her Morris Minor estate car.

The drive along the newly made road was a joy after the bumpy corrugations of the original track. She stopped at a view point Scatty had engineered into the side of the road on the edge of the escarpment. She drank her coffee and ate the sandwiches. Banana – she hadn't much else to use as a filling. Time to move on.

She turned off before she came to Scatty's camp as Con O'Hagan had said. There it was – a long, deep pit where the road makers had excavated soil to build the new surface. And there where the rain had moistened the earth was lovely, succulent gooey clay. Flora had taken great pains to demonstrate to her what kind her craft required and here it was in abundance.

She parked the Morris and took one of the buckets and the jembe. Looking down into the pit she could see it was much deeper than she had anticipated. On one side there were ridges which would serve as steps to get down to where she could mine the clay. Gingerly she clambered down to where she could see a seam. She drove the jembe into the soil and pulled lumps out to pack into the bucket. The last time she had done anything like this was when she had to move potatoes out of the clamp on the farm. She had mud and straw all over her clothing and her hands were scratched until they were rough. She had hated it and it was, she realised, the event that set her against farming. But it was the row with her father when she complained about it that made her adamant she was going to leave the farm as soon as she could.

The bucket of clay was heavier than she expected. She struggled with it as she tried to climb back up the side of the pit, making poor progress. She was so absorbed with this that she was unaware of anyone's presence. The voice calling *"Memsahib Deesee"* startled her. The African man standing high above her at the edge of the pit called out again. 'Memsahib. I need your help with Mister Scatty.'

With so few Europeans in the country Rosemary was not surprised the man knew who she was. She shielded her eyes to get a better view of him. Unlike most of the people she had seen on Elgon he was dressed in a white shirt and khaki shorts. His English was spoken with a mission school accent. 'Why do you need my help?'

'We found him very ill and we have brought him to his camp. He must be taken into the hospital and we have no motor car to take him. It would not be good for him on the back of a bicycle.'

If Scatty Muller was seriously ill of course she must help. She was determined to take the clay, too, even if she had only filled one bucket. The man climbed down to her and took the bucket, offering his hand to help her climb the last part. She had a feeling she had seen him somewhere before. He stood over six feet tall, broad shouldered and powerfully built. 'Where is Mr. Muller?' she asked.

'We found him in the bush and took him to his

camp. It is not far.'

The man sat in the passenger seat of her car as they drove back to the new road. About two miles on she saw the aluminium rondavels. She had never been this far before. She steered the small estate car towards the compound. The African said, 'Stop here, Memsahib Deesee.' Under a mango tree on a rough home made stretcher was a man. At first she wasn't sure if it was Muller, his clothes were so ragged and dirty. Three Africans stood nearby. She went closer. It was the road maker all right. But what a state he was in. A wound on his right leg was red and suppurating. He was unconscious and his breathing was laboured. She hardly dare look at the rest of his injuries. 'Do you know how long he has been like this?'

'No, Memsahib Deesee. We found him near the cave where the elephants go. He must have been in there. Maybe he was hit by an elephant.'

'I don't know that place. Where are his men? Shouldn't there be more than just the three of them?'

'That's all there are. The rest have left him. It is cruel of them. You see how bad he is. There is no-one else to help him. You must take him to Mbale.'

'I suppose that is all I can do. He should be able to lie flat in the back of my car.' Rosemary struggled with the catches to move the seats so that there was a clear space at the back, feeling foolish as the man came closer, peering at what she was doing. She pushed the empty buckets on one side and loaded the full one into the vehicle. Now came the task of moving Scatty Muller. It was going to be hard work and she felt her stomach heave as she looked at his wounds.

The African held Scatty round his shoulders, his hands gripping his clothing. 'You take his legs, Memsahib, and we can move him. She lifted his legs and grimaced as she came into contact with the pus from the wound. Between them they managed to lay the road foreman in the back of her car. She wiped her hands on a piece of cloth that covered the spare wheel. She turned to speak to the African but he was gone. There was so much more she wanted to ask him and she felt annoyed that she was denied this. She wanted to wash her hands but she couldn't see any water.

Rosemary began to panic. Everything felt wrong. She had to get away as quickly as she could. She knew she was driving too fast for the road conditions but she didn't care. The little car, designed and built for smooth English roads bounced and swayed over the bumpy track. She daren't look round to see Scatty as she was scared of bogging down in the poor surface. Reaching the new road would allow her to go faster. And faster she went, her stomach leaping as she hit the many bends at speeds that rocked her car, its wheels locking and sliding on the red earth surface as she braked too fiercely. She was shaking as she reached Mbale late in the afternoon, red dust covering her hair and streaking her sweating face.

She turned into Hospital Road and jumped from the car almost before it had stopped, climbing the flight of steps into the building in bounds. 'Slow down Rosemary, you'll overheat the pace you're going.' It was Sister McGregor. 'Dr. Cunningham is away until tomorrow,' she said after she had heard Rosemary's story. 'I'll get Mr. Muller in here where I can have a look at him. You go and make yourself a cup of tea in the kitchen.' Twenty minutes later the nurse emerged, frowning. 'I don't know what to make of him. He's still out. The wound is horrid and he has pustules breaking out over his body. Do you know what happened to him?'

'No, I've no idea other than an African says he was found by the cave where the elephants go, wherever that may be.'

'There's nothing more you can do here. Why don't you go home? I've some strong antiseptic. Wash your hands well with that before you go.'

'You make it sound serious. Is it?'

'I don't know. We'll only know when Dr. Cunningham gets back.'

The core members of the "Dini" summoned Juba to a meeting that night. Area Chief Erinayo's anger and contempt overflowed. 'You are a fraud. You have been telling us that we need to be bolder like the people of Mount Kenya, make more opportunities to show we mean business but you had the chance to do this today and what did you do? You got the DC's wife to take the Muzungu road maker to safety and to get well in Mbale. We had chased him all night. Because of what you have done we have wasted our time. You should have killed both of them.' Juba pulled his colobus skin cloak tighter round his shoulders. He knew that the senior "Dini" members would be sceptical. He stood and started to walk round behind the circle. He stopped and tapped the man next to Erinayo with his fly whisk.

'Why do you think I let the DC's woman take him to Mbale? Don't you think I had a reason?' The man shrugged his shoulder, at a loss to know what to say. Juba moved past Erinayo and leant over another man.

'Had the road maker been into the caves where the elephants go?'

'The man leant forward to distance himself from Juba. 'That is what I've heard said.'

'And has anyone here a long enough memory to recall what happened to people who went into that cave?'

Erinayo could feel his authority draining away. 'Of course we can. Everyone knows they became ill.'

60

Juba pointed his fly whisk at Erinayo. In the light of the fire it looked like a flaming torch. 'And did they recover?'

'No, they died. The Mganga's medicine was not strong enough.'

'They died.' Juba paused for effect. 'They died. And what happened to those who tried to help them?'

'Some of them died too.'

'Do you now see why I sent the DC's woman to Mbale with the road maker? I was careful to let her do most of the handling of Muller. She had his mess all over her. Like our people in the past she will not survive. The death is horrible as we know from our history. And other Wazungu in Mbale will die. Even the doctor and nurses who try to help Muller.' Juba could see he was winning. 'If I had killed them the polisi would come and there would be trouble for a lot of us. This way they will be uncertain what to do.' He knew he had won the majority over.

Erinayo did not give up. 'So some of the Wazungu die. How will this further our cause? They won't know this was our work.'

'When we are ready we will tell them.'

TEN

On top of Nakasero Hill in Kampala stood "The Fort". A relic of the early days of British exploration it now housed the Uganda Police Quartermaster's Stores. Bolts of khaki drill for uniforms, boots, puttees, headgear, belts, buttons, soap, books and forms, lots and lots of forms – if a police station needed it, it could be found in "The Fort". It was ideal for its purpose since its walls were high and thick and there was only one way in and one way out, through twelve feet tall wooden gates, studded with heavy iron bolts. Secure. Impenetrable.

George Bliss, the Quartermaster, had long experience of the responsibilities of his post, from his days in the British Army and then the Palestine Police. "The Fort" was his empire. All vehicles had to be parked in the appointed places well away from where the stores were kept. And well away from the armoury which was at the far end of the compound and backing on to the thickest wall.

Bliss arrived early. His schedule included the six monthly stock taking of the armoury and experience told him this would occupy most of the day. Maybe the whole day since his Head Armourer, Abou Bakr was off sick. A Comoran Arab, Abou had been employed in the armoury for longer than anyone could remember. Always clad in a rumpled white drill suit topped with a tasselled red fez he was the ideal armourer. As well as being technically efficient he understood the need for balance between security of his charges and the urgency with which they might be required. He was held as a model of efficiency and loyalty to anyone posted to "The Fort", whatever their length of service.

Bliss got through his daily routines of clearing mail

and wireless messages and signing the pile of requisitions from police Districts which his clerk placed before him – using his time honoured economy device of automatically reducing any indented amount by ten percent. He changed into his khaki dust coat ready for the armoury. He would follow his usual order – start with the Bren light machine guns, move on to the pistols and then the Force's reserve of rifles – 350 short magazine Lee Enfields, the standard issue to all units. And finally the check of the ammunition. This was always the longest part since all the heavy boxes had to be unscrewed and opened to verify the contents.

He summoned James Olumu, the Assistant Armourer. 'Have you got Abou's keys and the registers?' The African held a bunch of keys up and shook them. 'Good man. Let's get started.' The armoury was a long narrow building and with the rapid increase in the size of the Force since the riots in 1947 it was now cramped for space. First the Brens – they counted them, checked the serial numbers, removed the barrels and magazines to inspect them for cleanliness. All correct. They moved on to the pistols; rack after rack of Webleys, Remingtons and Smith and Wessons and by the time they had finished counting and checking the revolvers it was time for the mid-day break. 'That's enough for now, James. We'll do the ammunition and the rifles when we come back at thirteen hundred. Careful how you lock up.'

1.00 p.m. The rifles stood in their racks in seven rows of fifty. Chains passed through their trigger guards and were padlocked to staples concreted into the walls. This was the darkest part of a gloomy room, barely lit by four sixty watt light bulbs. 'Head count first, James,' and they both stood silently counting. 'How many do you make it?' Olumu licked his pencil and checked the tally he had made. '350, correct, sir.'

'I'm the same. Now the detail check.' Row by row the chains were removed. Serial numbers were noted, oil bottles and pull-throughs in the butt traps were inspected and they removed the bolts from a random sample and looked down the barrels. It was getting hot and airless and Bliss was glad to say, 'One more row and we're done.' But they weren't. The Quartermaster couldn't believe what he found in the back row. In place of twelve rifles there were twelve broomsticks. Each had the metal muzzle and bayonet casting from a normal rifle fitted on top so that with a quick inspection from a distance the numbers looked correct. 'Lock them all up, James. Don't touch any more. We'll do the ammunition. And look lively about it.'

It was back breaking work unscrewing every heavy wooden ammunition case, but it had to be done. One hundred and fifty rounds of .303 were missing. They checked the issues registers and then they checked them again. And still a hundred and fifty rounds were missing. Under normal circumstances Bliss would have written this off as issued for range practice without signature or one of the many other ways that Quartermasters have for concealing embarrassing shortages but this was no occasion for accounting sleight of hand. 'Give me all the registers and Abou's keys. I'll lock up. Don't leave until I tell you. I'll have to inform CID.'

Bliss didn't like the Assistant Commissioner in charge of CID. He thought of him as a jumped up detective sergeant from the London Metropolitan and this wasn't London. He had to ring him, knowing the response he would get.

'Well that's a good one, George ... broomsticks, eh. I'll have to look into this one myself. The Commissioner will have to be informed, of course.' He would, wouldn't he, thought the Quartermaster.

The CID Assistant Commissioner arrived with three African detectives. The enquiry carried on late into the evening. The ACP was prickly. Most evenings he enjoyed a steak and a few drinks at the Kampala Club and he was missing out. But this was too hot to leave.

He took over Bliss's office. He detailed the Scenes of Crime man to dust all the broomsticks and end castings for fingerprints and then he turned to Bliss. 'Let's have your staff roll,' and he went down the list with the detectives standing behind him. 'Nineteen men in total. One clerk, five drivers – all been in Stores for eight years or more- five storemen, three armoury staff and eight porters. Get them all in. My detectives will see them.'

Bliss didn't need to check, 'They're all here except for the Head Armourer, Abou Bakr. He's off sick.'

By the time the ACP called a halt to the enquiries the file was thick with statements without any information to show how – and when – the rifles had been taken. The staff had sound backgrounds, though these would have to be checked more thoroughly. As in all police units they came from tribes throughout the Protectorate – even as far afield as the Eastern and Northern Districts. He pinned his hopes on the fact that a key witness – Abou Bakr - still hadn't been seen. His evidence was vital.

Two detectives searched the warren of narrow streets in Old Kampala trying to find Abou Bakr's home. Eventually they found his rooms. There was no-one there. None of the neighbouring tenants had seen him that day. The CID chief now sat hunched close to the telephone in the Quartermaster's office. It was midnight before it rang. 'He's what … missing from his home? I thought he was sick. Have you tried the Hospital? … well keep at it … no excuses, you must

65

find him, tonight.

Late the following day the Head Armourer was found. He was face down in the Nakivubo channel, a deep rainwater gulley near to his home. He was still wearing the white drill suit and the fez was found in the rushes alongside the channel. It was hard to determine whether there were any marks of violence with the amount of flesh removed by animal bites. The post mortem examination showed he had died from drowning. Rumour circulated that Abou Bakr's unhealthy interest in young boys had become too apparent for his community and he had been pressured to finish this in any way he chose. The Sudden Death file stayed open for another six months when it was closed "Cause of death uncertain". The crime file, *Theft of Firearms from the Police Armoury*", was moved from desk to desk in Police Headquarters, no-one daring to close it since they would have to admit the crime was going to stay unsolved.

ELEVEN

The journey from Entebbe was nearly over. Woolly Bill and the Medical Officer were both tired after a long day of meetings. Heavy rain had slowed their progress down for the last thirty miles. Now the distant lights of Mbale were a welcome sight.

'I'm for a long soak in the bath with a nice cold whisky,' announced Woolly Bill as they reached the tarmac road of the Township. 'No doubt you'll be doing the same.'

'Later. I'll call in the hospital first to see what has happened during the day. Drop me off will you.'

Matt Cunningham climbed the steps to the front door of the hospital. At the end of the long veranda sat Sister McGregor, writing notes in files. She leapt up as soon as she saw the Medical officer. 'Am I glad to see you, Doctor Cunningham,' and before he could do anything else she rattled off the circumstances of Scatty Muller's admission. She ended with, 'I didn't know what to make of him so I put him in the isolation ward.'

Cunningham didn't have his whisky that night. He sat with Scatty Muller until 3.00a.m., worried about his temperature and coma. Sister McGregor had treated the wound and given a penicillin injection and he could do no more than keep Muller under observation.

He must have dozed off. It was light. He felt grubby and his mouth tasted foul. He was still in the chair in the isolation ward alongside Muller. The road maker was unconscious. Cunningham stretched and went out onto the verandah. It was 6.30 a.m. and the hospital was coming to life. Looking down from the verandah he could see the nurses moving around the open wards that housed African patients. He felt troubled. He didn't know what to make of Scatty. What was that old Latin saying - "Ex Africa semper aliquid novi"? Out of Africa always something new. That was certainly true of disease. He spotted Victoria Semliki the Senior Nurse, next in rank to Sister McGregor. It was said that she came from the local royal family and though no-one had ever confirmed this she had a certain regal poise as she moved through the wards. How long she had been at Mbale Hospital was lost in the mists of time but her far reaching memory was prized in a culture where expatriates moved on to other stations as they completed their three year tours of duty. Matt Cunningham quickened his stride and caught up with her. 'Victoria, no-one here knows Elgon as well as you do. What do you know of the diseases there?'

'It is what you would expect Doctor. On the lower parts of the mountain, malaria - as there is anywhere in Uganda. Septic sores and ulcers which take time to heal, tape worms, dysentery, tick fever. There was leprosy but that's under control now. The missionaries have helped with this.'

'What about higher up? Say at the level of the new road.'

'Not much malaria – the water is all running. Less dysentery, the water is clean. I should say there is good health higher on the mountain. The air is good. It makes people strong as well as helping to grow good coffee.'

'That's what I would have thought yet I have heard stories of people dying there of a strange disease. That was long before my time here. Do you know anything of this?'

'Oh yes. They still talk around the fire at night of hunters going into the cave of the elephants and swelling up and dying and people who touch them dying too.'

'Cave of the elephants? That sounds a bit far-

68

fetched. Is there really such a place? Do you believe the stories about the disease?'

'Most stories have some truth. It is said that they who deal in African medicine failed to stop the disease so they put a strong taboo on going to the cave. There were no more instances of the disease and the medicine men saved their faces.'

'Victoria, you have a memory like a cave full of elephants. Thank you.'

The Senior Nurse smiled regally and continued into the ward. Matt Cunningham hurried back to his office. He searched his filing cabinet and pulled out the World Health Organisation circular - information about the virus epidemic at Bumba in the Congo. He reminded himself of the symptoms - weakness, headaches sore throat, dry hacking cough, suppuration when blisters broke open - and that the incubation time could be as short as two days.

Anxiety gripped him as he read further - death was likely to occur within two weeks of contracting the disease. Handling a dead body even put others at risk. Had this virus been lurking in a cave on Elgon only to be held at bay by witch doctors' taboos? He reached for the phone and rang the District Game Officer. 'Thank goodness you're in. I'm coming over to see you...' He cut off the voice on the end of the line with a terse, 'It's very important.' He all but ran the half mile to the Game Department offices. He was wheezing from his exertions as he sat down in front of the Game Officer. 'Tim, do you know anything about elephants going into a cave on Elgon?'

'I didn't know you were into game, Matt. Thinking of getting a licence to go after ivory? If you are you'll have to get fit.'

'No winding up, please. This is serious.'

'OK. It's not something that many people know.

Elephants normally live in woodlands and they get their salt from the trees and the grass, but on this part of Elgon there is so much rain that the salt is leached out of the foliage. Somehow the Elgon elephants discovered that the walls of a cave are lined with salt – as far as I can find out it is only one particular cave. They troop a hundred yards or more into the mountainside every now and again and dig the salt from the walls with their tusks.'

'Does anything else go into the cave?'

'Not much. Some of the scavengers but the roof is lined with bats. Millions of them. That rings a bell – are you thinking this has something to do with the fever you mentioned at Woolly Bill's meeting?'

'I sincerely hope not, Tim. Keep this to yourself will you until I know more.'

When Cecil came in late the previous night Rosemary had found it difficult to tell him about Scatty Muller. He was full of enthusiasm for the new Governor and almost as soon as he had run his bath he started to tell her about his meeting with him. 'He's been appointed to steer Uganda towards Independence. He says the government were talking about a thirty year period before that happens. Still, that can wait until morning.' And now over the cornflakes she knew she must tell him. She broached the subject with, 'Scatty Muller is very ill.'

There was no response. She tried again. 'Cecil, did you hear what I said …'

'You said that Muller was ill. It happens. Is there anything special about his being ill?'

She related the events of the previous day. The recrimination she had anticipated about her going up Elgon never came. Instead he said, 'I want Matt to examine you.'

'It's not me that's ill.'

'From what you described whatever he has got is very serious. You don't know what is wrong with him. For all we know if might be catching. You must have touched him when you got him into the car.'

'Of course I did but I think you're going over the top …'

'No I'm certainly not. We're going to see Matt right now.'

The examination was brief. The District Medical Officer hardly wanted to admit he didn't know what he was looking for. He just followed the list of symptoms in the WHO bulletin. He found nothing but he couldn't take a chance – it was early days. 'Cecil, burn all the clothes Rosemary was wearing yesterday. She's going to have to stay here in the isolation ward until I know a bit more.'

With Rosemary in the ward the Medical officer took the DC to his office. After he had covered what he knew of the "Elgon disease" – as he had started to call it – he confessed, 'I'm at a loss to know what is wrong with Scatty. He's still out for the count so we don't really know what happened to him. The Sister says he was covered in muck which smelled as though it might have been bat droppings but we don't know if he has been anywhere near the cave. And that WHO circular... four hundred dead ...' The Medical Officer couldn't finish the sentence. The thought of such an epidemic in his District was beyond consideration.

TWELVE

As soon as he heard about Scatty Muller Charles Harkness hurried to the hospital. Sister McGregor ignored his indignant outbursts at being kept out of the Isolation Ward but she allowed him to peer from the verandah through the net-curtained window. Even though he could see little of his Road Foreman it was clear he would get no information from him yet. He knew that Muller was normally capable of looking after himself, and his men too for that matter. Judging by the state of him something had gone dramatically wrong at the camp. Since the Road Foreman could tell him nothing yet there was only one thing to do. Go and see what he could find out. He collected his watchman – you never know when you will need pushing out of a mud slick – and set off.

It was some time since he had seen the later stages of the new road. Its quality was very impressive. Muller certainly knew how to get a good job done with his gang of Africans and a few pieces of plant that were well past their prime. He just hoped he wouldn't be in hospital too long. What he had seen gave him a feeling of optimism. There were deadlines for finishing the road but once Scatty was back on his feet, well who knew what might be achieved. He came to the end of the new section and now was bumping along the old track. He could see the aluminium rondavels ahead. He turned into the compound to be met by smoke-blackened machinery with burnt out tyres and the sight of all the forty-four gallon petrol and diesel barrels holed and drained. There was no cause for optimism now.

He climbed out of the Land Rover and made his way towards the rondavels. The foul stench hit him long before he reached the first one. He had no need to open the door to know where the smell came from. He could only just make out that the object dangling from the lamp hook, pulsating with maggots, was a dog's carcase. Sickened by what he was experiencing he reached in his pocket for his handkerchief and tripped over Simba's head on the floor. What the hell had really happened to Muller?

He heard the voice call for him. As he came out into the sunlight he recognised Scatty's Headman, Odoi. Then he saw several other men, whom he knew as gangers, half hidden but peering out from behind the blackened road grader. Odoi carried a short spear and a panga hung from his belt.

The Headman's account started with the Thompson's gazelle and the wonderful pay day braai. How it all changed after they had gone to their huts to sleep. Men armed with spears and a razor sharp panga held to his throat. Being told that he and all the other men in the camp should disappear and not come back. He showed Harkness the fresh scar on his neck as supporting evidence. 'There were many of them and we were not prepared for a fight and so we all ran into the bush.' Harkness took it for granted that the amount of alcohol they had each drunk had rendered them incapable of self-defence. 'Then I heard them calling out Bwana Scatty's name and saying they were going to kill him. Bwana Scatty left the camp too. I don't know where he went. But after many hours some men came and found me and took me down the mountainside and there was Bwana Scatty lying on the ground. I noticed his rifle in the long grass and covered it over. Now there were three more of our gang there. We had to carry Bwana Scatty on branches back to our camp. He still hadn't woken up.'

Harkness had not anticipated such disarray. Not

only did he have a very sick Road Foreman, he had no
working equipment. Road rollers, dumper trucks and
graders were not easy to come by. Those damaged here
were brought all the way from the ill-fated Groundnuts
Scheme in Tanganyika. And that was no longer a
source of supply. Maybe his foreman mechanic,
Bansilal, could work his usual miracles. But what was
worse was whether the gang would stay here. Odoi
appeared to have read Harkness's mind. 'It could not
happen that way again,' said the Headman. 'We have
spears and clubs. We will stay here and look after the
camp. None of *my* gang will leave.' Harkness's initial
anger damped down. No Road Foreman, no plant, but
at least there was a gang – one tribe sticking together.
Before he set out on the return journey to Mbale he
promised Odoi rations and other stores. Now he had to
see Woolly Bill and Tug quickly. Did they know the
strength of this? He doubted it.

The first mile of his journey was on the old track
before it was transformed into Scatty's new road.
Harkness drove carefully watching the surface ahead.
The watchman suddenly grabbed Harkness's shoulder.
'Men - spears - edge of bush …' There was a log across
the road a hundred yards ahead. He stopped the vehicle.
There was no way round the obstacle – thick bush on
one side and a drop of hundreds of feet down the
escarpment on the other. He rammed the knob to select
four wheel drive and put his foot down as hard as he
could on the accelerator and the Land Rover jumped
forward gripping the loose black cotton soil of the
track. It was no use hitting the tree trunk in the middle.
It had to be at one end and spin it round. He was aiming
at the end nearest the bush when he saw the rock. Take
that route and he would smash the radiator, sump and
God knows what else. To the right he could see the
drop and he felt the wave of vertigo grip him. He

closed his eyes as the reinforced bumper of the vehicle rammed the obstacle. He screamed as he felt the rear wheels slipping towards the edge.

The traction of the four wheel drive saved them from the fatal drop down the escarpment. The vehicle scraped past the log, its wheels swirling up dust. As it slowed one of the men from the bush jumped into its back. Only thick canvas separated the truck body from the cab. The spear jabbed through the canvas grazing the watchman's face. The watchman grabbed the spear's shaft and pulled hard and then rammed it back with all the force he could find. In his rear view mirror Harkness saw the man' sprawling figure hit the dusty track as he fell over the tail board.

It was several miles before Harkness felt it safe to stop. With the watchman wearing a plaster from the first aid kit over the cut on his face he drove on down the new road with a heavy clunking noise from the nearside front wheel. The rest of the journey, though he had to travel gingerly, was uneventful. He made for the police station as soon as he arrived in the Township.

'So, it's started,' said Wilson when he heard Harkness's story. 'The question is just how big will it get? Let's see if Woolly Bill is in.' Ten minutes later they were sitting in front of the DC's desk.

'I guess we all felt something like this was coming. I suppose they thought hitting Muller and his crew first would make the right impact – a European working for government with a gang of outsiders. I think road making is on hold for a while, Charles. What do you want to do, Tug?'

'I'll send Inspector Gurbachan Singh to investigate the incident at Scatty's camp. That's got to be the starting point. At the same time I'll have an armed patrol further up Elgon. They'll be doing no more than showing the flag but there's a chance they will pick up some useful information. That will stretch my resources so I'll put what I've got left on stand-by down here.'

Wilson saw Woolly Bill's frown. 'You said an armed patrol. I'm not keen on firearms at this stage. The sight of guns always tends to escalate things. I still think most of the people on Elgon don't support trouble of this kind.'

Tug stared at the DC. The memory of his wounds in Palestine when he was blown up by an Israeli booby-trap while trying to collect the bodies of British soldiers lynched in an olive grove was as vivid in his mind as ever. There must have been people there who didn't support that kind of violence but he'd never found a way of knowing who they were. 'You don't know the strength of it, nor do I. I'll make a concession. They'll take rifles but keep them racked in the vehicles until the inspector decides his men should be armed. It will be his decision. Until then they will be armed with shields and riot batons. They are going to be naked without something to show they mean business.'

'I suppose that will have to do. I shall stay here. Are you going yourself?'

'Not yet. I want to get a better feel of what is happening. Inspector Lingard will take a patrol to find out the size of it. Inspector Gurbachan Singh will investigate what happened at Scatty Muller's camp and then join up with Lingard. With a bit of luck …' Tug left his sentence unfinished.

THIRTEEN

The battered Dodge pick-up truck bumped along the track to Mbale station. Porters lounged on the cotton bales stacked on the loading platform and eyed the vehicle's arrival with lack of enthusiasm. The covered goods wagon, which had brought consignments transhipped at Tororo Junction from various locations, had arrived three days earlier. It had been offloaded that morning and its contents removed to the bowels of the building.

The Indian goods clerk, Ramesh, had seen the African before. He had called three days running enquiring if his goods had arrived. The invoice had shown a name only– Sitanuli Muchanga - and no address. This wasn't unusual on the rare occasions that a consignee was an African. Few had postal addresses so no delivery could be made as was the case of the Asian traders within the Township.

'They have come, two cases.' He looked through the papers on his clipboard and then beckoned the man to come into the shed. He pointed to the stacks of goods. 'Go in and look for the marks KLA/336-2/MBL.' The man shook his head. Ramesh sighed. Another one who can't read. He moved around the shed, eventually finding the consignment under a bundle of car exhaust pipes. Two wooden crates marked "Machinery parts". The man made his thumbprint on the delivery note. Ramesh witnessed it, writing "Right Thumb Mark of Consignee" and the man departed with his consignment.

The Dodge pick-up found the going hard as it hit the higher reaches of Scatty's road. The exhaust belched smoke and the clutch slipped. Still Sitanuli drove on. He didn't know what was in the crates. He only knew that General Elgon had told him to go and collect them. If anyone had asked him at the station he was to say they were parts for his coffee drying plant. That he had let this slip into disrepair beyond help was immaterial. He had been angry because the Coffee Co-operative Muzungu had told him that he would get no more money until he had saved enough from what he had earned instead of spending it on drink and women.

He was tempted to stop and have a look inside one of the crates. What was so important that he had to drive all the way to the station? After all they were addressed to him. On second thoughts, maybe not. Look what happened to Mbuzi. He had reached the road maker's camp and look what they had done here.

He arrived at the end of the road. Now it was a rutted track, barely passable for the Dodge. This was where General Elgon had said he should take the load. He pulled up alongside the water where the first of the several falls on the Sipi River plunged. The falling water pounding away from a hundred or more feet above had carved a deep cave behind the waterfall. It was possible to enter it without even getting soaked if care was taken in walking along a narrow ledge behind the torrent. Now he would just have to wait until General Elgon appeared. With difficulty he pulled both of the crates from the Dodge and sat on one of them.

It was nearly dark when General Elgon arrived. 'You have done well, Sitanuli. Now we will carry them where I want them.' He pointed to the cave. He got the expected protests but took no notice. They struggled with the first crate. Sitanuli had enough difficulty while they were on the river's bank that General Elgon feared they would never get both of them into the cave. It was only through his strength that they managed to stow the big boxes in the deepest part.

'They were heavy, what is in them,' asked Sitanuli.

General Elgon had no alternative but to get him to collect the boxes from the station but he had no respect for Sitanuli nor did he trust him. 'That's not for you to know. You will find out when the time is right. Now you should go. And keep quiet about this.' He contemplated whether Sitanuli should follow Mbuzi. Wait and see, he said to himself, we might need his vehicle again.

Once he could no longer hear the sound of the pickup General Elgon took his panga and gently prised the lid off one of the boxes. First there was a layer of sacking material. He pulled this aside and there lying neatly packed were the rifles. James had done a good job. The guns no longer looked like weapons soldiers or the police used. The woodwork of their barrels had been neatly cut back giving them the appearance of sporting rifles. They were lighter and easier to handle. He checked the second crate and found the ammunition packed under the weapons. Now he could show them the power he had promised, the sort of power they had never expected. The power to make the "Dini" feared. He collected debris that had been washed into the mouth of the cave and covered the crates. As he inched his way across the ledge to the bank of the river he nursed one of the rifles. He smiled as he lifted it to his shoulder and felt its weight.

The inner circle of the Dini ya Mungu Wetu waited. Impatiently. Word had gone round that General Elgon had important news. But he wasn't there yet. The muttering started. He was a fraud, he wasn't as committed as he said he was. Why had he been to Kenya? Because he was going to go there and abandon them. After all, he may have been born on Elgon but he wasn't really one of them was he? Feelings were running high by the time he appeared.

'What is it you want to tell us that is so big?' It was

Erinayo that spoke. He felt that it was now time for his bid for leadership.

General Elgon did not walk round behind the circle as he usually did. He needed centre stage for this. He wore his cloak. He stood, legs astride , in front of them. The flames of the fire picked out his muscular frame. 'This is what I wanted to show you. I promised power. Here it is.' He pulled the rifle from under his cloak and held it high above his head. The gasps were loud.

FOURTEEN

The gap between terms at the College was too long for Con O'Hagan. No students had returned yet and there were few members of the teaching staff on the campus. He had done all the maintenance and building work that had been waiting for the break and he had prepared teaching material for the new term. Now what?

He sat daydreaming on the veranda outside the gymnasium where he still trained those students who had a taste for boxing. He rocked back in his chair, put his feet up on the verandah rail and clasped his hands behind his head. Some of the boys showed potential but none came any where near the tall young man with the smouldering temper. What had happened to him, he wondered. Wanyama. What was his other name? Juba, that was it.

The priest still blamed himself for his prize student walking out. He knew the arguments Juba had made. He had been over them often enough with other Africans who had passed through the College. Intelligent boys all of them, they had been encouraged to debate issues and to think for themselves. But in the end none had openly rejected the religion that had nursed them through an education in a country where education was a rare and precious commodity. All of those he could recall had gone on to good jobs. Why, two were now lawyers and heading for the heights in politics. He should – could – have talked Juba round. And the boxing. It would have been the championships, maybe the Olympics and who knows what else.

Ah well, spilt milk and all that. So now what?

He had been so busy in the last term that he was out of touch with what was happening in the Township. Maybe he should go and see Rosemary and find out how her newly learned language was working and catch up on the local gossip. It had been refreshing working with her. He had nothing to replace the early mornings hammering away at structure, intonation and vocabulary. And her passion for what she was doing. He phoned the DC's house number. It was a long time ringing. He was about to give up when an African voice answered. 'Memsahib Deesee isn't here,' was all he could get. Why did he feel so disappointed? He would go over to the house any way. He could take Flora a gift of clay. She was always there, or so it seemed, and that would give him first hand knowledge of how Rosemary was getting on with the language. If that was what he really wanted to know?

Con O'Hagan's means of transport was a 350cc BSA motor cycle. An ex-military workhorse which a Sergeant of the British army - a Belfast Catholic - stationed at Tororo had passed on to him with a nod and wink when the unit pulled out in 1949. With his aptitude for anything mechanical he had no difficulty in refurbishing all the bits that mattered. It looked a wreck but ran like a dream.

As he turned into the driveway to the Woodley-Will's house he spotted Flora grinding maize outside her quarters. And there near her was the oven Rosemary had acquired. He parked the motor cycle and strode over to the woman, greeting her as he went. Flora looked up and smiled welcomingly. The smile broke into a huge beam as he handed her the clay. He squatted down beside her and as he talked she responded with the sign language that he and Rosemary had worked out with her.

He realised that he had never had a close look at the work produced by the woman, the work that Rosemary so enthused over. 'You have become quite famous for the little people that you make. I was wondering if you would show me some of them.' Flora stood up and beckoned to him to follow her into her quarters. There on a book case Rosemary had given her were rows of statuettes and busts. In the gloom of the small room he could not see them clearly. Flora noticed this and took six of them and stood them outside on the concrete. There fixing him with the gaze he knew so well, draped in a colobus skin cloak, was Juba. He knew from Rosemary that Flora had the remarkable ability to sculpt accurately from memory but he would never have believed that anyone could do this with such precision and indeed truth. Staring at him was an even stronger picture of arrogance than when Juba had walked out of the College.

'Where was this man when you saw him?'

'On Elgon,' said her signed answer.

'When did you make this?' he asked pointing to the statuette. She replied through her signs that it was recently made. 'Was that the last time you saw him?'

Flora shook her head and signed. 'No. That was just before the last long rains.' O'Hagan realised that was well before the woman had been brought there by Woodley-Wills. Now he had to know more, things he doubted he could find out from her. Back at the College was Brother Sebastian, a local man with a deep understanding of Elgon and its people. Con O'Hagan thanked Flora and set out for the College.

He was in luck. Sebastian was there. Yes, he knew of a young man who had stirred up the members of the "Dini". Yes, from the description it could be Juba though they did not call him that now. "General Elgon" was the name he had adopted and used. It followed the pattern of names being used by the organisation on Mount Kenya. And yes, he did know the area where he could usually be found.

Con O'Hagan could never have explained why he

made the decision to ride his motor cycle up the road to Mount Elgon. He filled it with petrol and set off. He knew where he was going but he had no plan other than he must see Juba Wanyama – or whatever he called himself. The priest was known around Mbale for keeping to a sedate speed but now, white cassock billowing out, throttle wide open, he rode as he had never ridden before. As he rode he rehearsed what he would say to the man when they met. He reached the foothills and the new road was suddenly steeper. The bike laboured to maintain the speed. He still climbed. The engine pinked badly, the higher altitude enriching the petrol mixture, starving it of the air it needed. It was only then he was aware that he had been travelling for two hours and that it was already afternoon. He had to continue. And if he was too late to return that night he could always sleep rough.

Now he must turn off the well made road. From here on it would be rough tracks, some no more than game trails. He reached the first land mark, a clearing surrounding the local chief's offices. He stopped his motor bike. His eyes were watering – he had no goggles – and he couldn't see clearly. At first he saw only a few people standing near the building and then he realised it was burning. There were bodies lying nearby. The few had grown to a host, some carrying spears and pangas. He was surrounded, pulled roughly from the motor cycle. The machine fell on its side and he smelled the petrol as it decanted from the tank onto the ground. Now was the test of his command of the local language. 'I have come in peace. It does not matter to me what you have done here.'

The mob milled closer around him. A bearded man brandishing a short spear pressed his face close up to O'Hagan's. 'There is no peace here, Mzungu. The war has started.'

The chanting had begun. He now had to shout to make himself heard. 'I came to see General Elgon. Let me talk to him.'

'It won't make any difference whatever you have to say to him.'

Con O'Hagan could feel the growing pressure from the crowd. The preliminaries before going into battle; the smell of cannabis and the locally distilled strong drink. These gave the warriors the feeling there was all the time in the world to aim and throw a spear, load and shoot an arrow, swing a club. These intensified courage to the extent that they knew no limits. The situation was much worse than he had first thought. He tried again. 'I have come all this way in peace. Let me see General Elgon.'

The bearded man motioned to others in the crowd. 'Bring him. He shall see General Elgon if General Elgon wants to see him.' The priest was cordoned off by a group of armed men. They did not hold him but kept their formation around him. He had no option but to keep pace with them. When he slowed he felt the jab of a spear. He started to count his steps. Eight hundred … nine hundred … what was the point other than giving his mind something to do. Still they marched on, still climbing. They stopped. They had passed through the heavily wooded area and now he could see the remnants of the sun glinting on the peak of Wagagai. They were alongside a cave in the volcanic rock.

The armed men stood back. There in front of him was Juba Wanyama, a full scale version of what he had seen when he was with Flora. The man who had been a boy at the College stood in front of him. Drawn up to his full height and with his colobus skin cloak he was a commanding figure. He eyed the priest just as he had all those years ago when he had been taken to task for breaking his boxing training routine. 'They tell me you

85

want to see me. Why?'

'I have heard some of the things that are happening. For the sake of the people here I have come to plead with you to put a stop to this …'

'You can have nothing important to say to me now. You told me all I needed to know when I left the College.'

'What do you mean?'

'Come over here.' He pointed towards the cave. 'I will show you something.'

There was just enough light left for the priest to see the two crates, now without lids. Juba bent down and emerged slowly from the cave holding a rifle in each hand. He waved them above his head. 'Get guns, that was the gospel according to Father Con. I have done that.'

'You have twisted my words. You know that is not what I said. So you have a few guns. The police have many more. And even if by some miracle you hold them off the army will come with many more.'

'They will not expect us to have guns… when everyone sees that we are armed they will join with us as never before …'

'Don't you realise what you will be doing to those people …'

'It will not be me. It will be what you told me … an alien power doing it. We shall win, you will see.'

'He won't see anything, General Elgon. The dead can't see.' The man with the beard had stepped forward. 'It's all words. It's time for action. He pointed to the priest's cassock, now torn and smeared with mud. 'He wears the uniform of the enemy.'

Con O'Hagan looked around. The attention of the group of men was now on Juba and the bearded man. Some were squatting; some were leaning against the old twisted fig tree that stood near the cave. He didn't count them. He didn't want to know the odds. *Golden Gloves New Jersey 1926. Semi finals. He'd lost because of his Irish temperament. He was older and wiser now. He shuffled forward. He could hear the bell at the ringside. Keep your cool, Con, man. Keep your cool.*

The uppercut only travelled eighteen inches but it took the bearded man on the chin. He staggered and collapsed. Con O'Hagan could feel the shock of the punch all the way up his arm. He ripped what was left of the cassock from his body and now stood in singlet and shorts. *It felt right. He was in the ring again. And this time ... everything to fight for.* He shuffled forward. *He had always been proud of his footwork. Like a ballroom dancer they had said.* He feinted and sent in his right cross. Contact. But glancing. He swung in again, a triple combination of punches. Another man down.

And now the Dublin street fighter of his youth took over. His head butt smashed the nose of the man nearest him as he came forward. He swung round directly in front of Juba. *Oh, he knew the lad's weakness alright. Make him angry, stir him up.* Con O'Hagan danced as he had never danced before and mouthed the crudest of insults from the back streets of Ireland's capital. Understood by anyone. Anywhere. Juba – General Elgon, whoever – came flailing, just as the Irishman had anticipated.

A left feint and his famed right cross would do it.

The blow on the back of neck sent him reeling to what would have been the canvas. *Down, listen to the count, Con, don't come up too early Keep your eye on your corner for the signal from your second.*

There was no count, no safe haven of a corner. The bearded man swung the club again and "The Battling Mick" was out of the contest. For good. But this time not for the want of the right temperament.

FIFTEEN

'Superintendent Wilson, who's calling?'

'John Thompson, Special Branch, Kenya Police.' The telephone call came as a surprise.

'I'm at Tororo station. We've got a special train parked here. I have something you ought to know. I don't want to say anything more on the phone. Can you get over here?'

What was a Kenya police officer doing in a railway carriage at Tororo? Busy as he was Tug Wilson had no option but to go and see him. As he drove he puzzled over this but he had reached no conclusion when he arrived. There were two carriages and a dining car which had been shunted onto the goods siding, away from the main station. There was someone in the dining car motioning to him.

They were soon down to business. 'I've been travelling the line from Nairobi with this crew.' Thompson nodded towards a group of Africans who were sitting at the other end of the dining car, out of earshot. 'Until very recently they were active members of the subversive movement but have turned "loyalist". I won't go into the reasons why – but to tell you the truth I wouldn't want to go into the forests with them which is what some of our guys have to do.'

'Travelling the line and doing what?'

'We know that most of the tea stalls at the railway stations all the way from Nairobi to the border with Uganda are run by members of that organisation. It's a communication channel as well as a route for passing on members of the organisation taking a rest from the forests. On our way up the men we've brought with us have identified several important people and now they say there are two here in Tororo. We never anticipated

88

this or I would have been in touch earlier. We had to come to Tororo to turn round to go back ... '

'These important people your men have identified, what are they supposed to be doing here?'

'One of them holds the license for the Railway tea stall and is doing what the others are doing all along the line. The other man helps him, not only on the tea stall. I believe you have a community of their tribe living near here.'

'Yes, in Nyangole village. It comes right up to the railway line. We're actually sitting in Nyangole now. I know there is a lot of them – don't ask me how many. My Special Branch say they are mainly people who have got away from the troubles down your way and don't want any part of it.'

'Well, that's where these two come in.' Thompson took three photos from a file. They were all of a dead black and white cat hanging from a tree in what looked like a forest glade. It was just possible to see that the animal had been disembowelled. 'These were taken somewhere near here by a person from this locality and sent to us. Do you know what this is?'

'I could make a guess, but you tell me.'

'This is part of the paraphernalia of a second degree forest oath.'

'Meaning?'

'The Africans we brought with us say this is evidence that someone has been trying to intimidate people to join the movement in Kenya. Probably not to go back there but to start activities up here. And one of the commitments after taking the oath is to kill a European.'

'You think the tea stall holder is responsible for this?

'That's what those here say. They have identified him as an important man in the movement. He calls himself Fulani, but that's only "Whatsisname" in Swahili. We haven't got a name for the other one.'

'That's all I need just now. We have trouble reported on Mount Elgon and I have men going up there tomorrow morning.'

'You'll arrest these two, of course.'

'That's not so easy. You have an Emergency declared in Kenya. We don't – and I hope we never shall. Since there's no evidence of an offence being committed I can't arrest them. If you wanted to we'd have to get a warrant from the High Court. That would take days.'

'We're scheduled to go back late tonight. I could just lift them and no-one would be the wiser.'

'That's not on. You'll have to leave it with me and I will find out what I can do.'

'I hope you understand the gravity of what I'm telling you. Your trouble on Elgon might just be a local matter but it probably won't be much longer. Still, on your head be it. Let me give you a word of warning. Now there has been an oathing ceremony here you had better check if anyone has house servants from that tribe. If so, tell them to watch out. In Kenya a four year old European boy was beheaded by a house servant who had been with the family since before the child was born. He used to play with him, stick Elastoplasts on his scratches and so on. When he was arrested he confessed that he had just taken the oath.'

While the two police officers were still talking one of the "loyalists" on the train managed to get word to Fulani that he had been recognised. The Kenyan packed a few things from the back of the tea stall into a bundle, signalled to his compatriot and slowly walked out of the tea stall by its back door. They left the railway station without being seen from the dining car of the Special Train.

SIXTEEN

Inspector Gurbachan Singh set out with some apprehension. He had served in the army in India before coming to Uganda and what he had seen there during the build up to Partition, and particularly after it, made him no stranger to unimaginable violence. This had left him with an anger that sometimes felt uncontrollable. He often asked himself could anything like that happen here? And the answer always came back 'Why not?' Maybe not on the same scale but here the tribal differences were pronounced and this was interlaced with beliefs that were incompatible. Now, he told himself, I must put that beside me. It mustn't distract me from what I'm good at – investigation. This was a straightforward case of malicious damage and probably attempted murder and he and the men he was taking with him – two detectives, a sergeant and three constables all packed into the Ford Thames Trader police truck – were here for that purpose.

Harkness had told him of the damage to the plant and equipment and had been even more graphic about the attempt on his life during his drive back to Mbale. As they pulled into the camp's compound he was faced with a group of twenty men armed with an array of spears, pangas and cudgels. A tall man with tribal scars etched into his face stood facing them, a rifle slung over his shoulder.

The constables leapt from the vehicle, Greener shotguns at the ready. To their surprise the man with the rifle yelled, 'Don't shoot; we are Bwana Scatty's men, the Peeda road gang. I am the Headman, Petero Odoi.' He looked around and realised why the guns were pointing at them. 'We have armed ourselves in case they come back.'

91

'What are you doing with a gun?' called Gurbachan.

'It is Bwana Scatty's. I found it at the place where he was ill – the cave of the elephants. I am going to look after it until he comes back to us.' It didn't take the Sikh inspector long to verify that this was indeed the road gang, all from the same tribe and not from the Elgon area. The first part of his investigation was now going to be easier than he thought. And if Petero Odoi looked after the rifle it would save some paper work.

The Inspector started his enquiries. His two detectives questioned Odoi and his men and the five uniform constables patrolled the perimeter of the camp. By early afternoon the scene had been surveyed and sketch maps drawn. Simba's blood was still an ugly dark stain on the rondavel floor, the start of Scatty Muller's journey of horror.

From the statements taken there were sketchy descriptions of some of the raiders. These were of little help in identifying most of them but the name "General Elgon" figured as the leader of the party. This was a new name for Gurbachan and his policemen. Who was this man? None of the road gang knew anything more about him.

Now he had to concentrate on finding this "General". Gurbachan knew how difficult it was to get information on this part of the mountain and there was word that more trouble was starting. He would need to join forces with Lingard's patrol – safety in bigger numbers. He had to get to the rendezvous point at the compound of one of village chiefs.

While Gurbachan was setting out for the road maker's camp Lingard had gone to an area some five miles to the North East where several villages sprawled over the mountain's mid ground. The tracks were poor, rutted, and recent storms had washed away the loose soil and uprooted trees. "Get up there and show the flag, find the strength of what is happening, and report back," had been Tug Wilson's instructions, a little vague for Lingard's liking. Eighteen months earlier, before coming to Uganda as an Inspector, Police Constable Lingard had walked and cycled the streets of a market town in the Midlands of England. For much of the time "shaking hands with door-knobs" was the most exciting thing he did and he could hardly begin to compare this with the variety of work and people he met now. He had a sergeant and twelve men in a Ford Thames Trader truck. Ten rifles and two Greener heavy gauge shotguns were locked under the seats in the back. Wicker shields and heavy wooden riot batons were piled in a corner.

So far the journey had been quiet. They had stopped at each of the three villages they reached and Lingard made a show by parading his men in the more open spaces. Apart from there being a reluctance of anyone to speak to them they had seen and heard nothing untoward. They approached the next village through plantations of maize, sorghum and bananas. Still no change from what they had experienced so far. Until they entered the clearing. What had been the local chief's office was still a smouldering ruin. There was no-one to be seen. The sergeant sent constables to the nearest houses. After a time they returned with half a dozen villagers. There was the usual language difficulty but at last they found a man who spoke English. 'We didn't want this trouble. It is the Dini. They have stirred up our people.'

'Where is everyone,' asked Lingard.

'They have gone further up the mountain. Something is happening there. I don't know what it is but they have gone. It must be something important they must see because the Dini said we would all suffer

93

if they did not go. Some of them want to join the Dini but most are afraid and scared not to go. That is all we know.'

As he finished speaking Gurbachan Singh arrived. He told Lingard about Scatty's camp and General Elgon. 'Let's see if they know anything about this man.' He turned to the villager. 'Do you know a man who is called General Elgon?'

The reluctance showed on the man's face. With the arrival of Gurbachan and his party the police numbers were more formidable and Gurbachan was a fearsome figure with his heavy brows and nose like an eagle's beak. 'Well, do you?'

'Yes. Everyone knows about General Elgon. He is important in the Dini.'

'Where is he now?'

The man said nothing but pointed with his chin towards the track that led out of the village and further up Elgon. 'So that is where we have to go,' said Gurbachan. 'If he is anywhere to be found we cannot leave without him. There is plenty of evidence to connect him with the raid on Muller's camp.'

Lingard felt buoyant. Now it was going to be a bit more than "flying the flag". Gurbachan leant out of the window of his vehicle. 'It will pay us not to be complacent. I'd make sure your firearms are available. Mine are.'

'Tug said to keep them out of sight until it was really necessary ...'

'Who knows when necessary may be? Let's go,' was the Sikh's response.

The two police vehicles moved off out of the clearing and onto the track. Gradually all signs of habitation were left behind. The vehicles' engines laboured. The landscape became rocky – sharp edged volcanic rock with small caves burrowing into the hillside. The track narrowed and was harder to negotiate. Suddenly they were upon the clearing. The noise of the engines had preceded them and a sea of faces a hundred yards in front of them turned to look at the police party.

The truck in which Lingard rode stopped, forcing the following vehicle to pull in behind. He called to Gurbachan. 'There's something going on up there but it doesn't look like trouble. If you stay here I'll take some men and go and see what's happening.' Lingard still had something of the English "Bobby" about him. He looked as though he was about to walk around the local cattle market or at worst to a pub fight on a Saturday night.

'Firearms? Batons?' queried Gurbachan.

'Let's not provoke anything.'

The Sikh raised his bushy eyebrows. Lingard set off with his men. Crowds of Africans were nothing new to him. He had policed partisan football matches with their huge followings in Kampala. This looked like any other crowd. It was quiet. No show of weapons. His best estimate was several hundreds. He could just make out a tall man standing on a hillock, addressing the throng. From that distance he could not hear his words. The crowd seemed passive, attentive to what the man was saying. Lingard stopped and weighed up the possibilities. There was no sensible route through them. The area was a shallow basin with a rocky perimeter and a path-like route round the edge where he and his policemen would be just above the crowd. That was his route. He and his men clambered up the rocky slope.

With the extra height Lingard could see the man on the hillock turning to face a huge fig tree near the mouth of a small cave. A rumbling noise began to echo from the people assembled. It rose to a crescendo and then suddenly stopped. Their attention was held by the

95

tree, some spectacle that he couldn't yet see. His policemen eased themselves further along the perimeter. At last he saw what it was. The man had pulled a blanket away and Con O'Hagan's cruciform body, nailed to the fig tree, appeared to be looking down on them all.

This was like no football match, no market place, nothing Lingard had ever witnessed before. He was whipped into full consciousness by the man on the hillock and the grizzly spectacle in front of him. He could see his monkey skin cloak now. He was shaking a large fly whisk in the direction of the policemen. He heard the crowd as one voice chant the name "General Elgon". They were turning towards them.

The first rifle shots were high. They brought spatters of red rocky chippings down behind Lingard. The crowd roared. Cheered. It was the first time they had heard the sound of the new power General Elgon had brought to them. More shots. Lingard knew they had to get back to the safety of the vehicles. Fast. He knew too that the man Gurbachan hunted was in front of them. The next shot hit a corporal in his right leg, blood spurting out from under his blue puttees. The following shot hit a rock. The ricocheting bullet, now transformed into a lethal piece of jagged metal, sliced into Lingard's throat. He fell and the constables struggled to move their inspector and corporal to a safer place. There were still more shots but they flew high over the heads of the police party.

Gurbachan Singh had ordered the issue of rifles, shotguns and riot equipment before the first of the shots. He had organised his men into two parties – one armed with batons and shields and the other with firearms. He took charge of the baton party himself. All of the policemen were from Northern tribes – Acholi and West Nile men, tall, strong and in every way different from the people of Elgon. They raced towards the perimeter where Lingard was being carried along by two constables. Another constable was supporting the corporal who was hobbling slowly. The crowd, sensing an easy kill, started to surge in that direction too. The first shots from the Greener guns, loaded with heavy buckshot, slowed the host's advance. The next shots turned them, giving Gurbachan the chance to reach Lingard. He heaved the European onto his shoulders and at a sharp trot headed for the vehicles. The sergeant had picked up the corporal and was alongside the Sikh as they reached the first tender.

The baton party, covered by the armed police, reached the vehicles where the drivers were already revving their engines furiously. Gurbachan could see the man he wanted. He was still standing on the hillock haranguing the crowd, urging them to attack the police. The Sikh Inspector wanted him badly. With the men at his disposal – better trained in the use of firearms than anyone who had fired on them – he could drive his way through the mob. He could see them clearly now, mainly men but there were also a few women, some bearing children on their backs. He must take some action otherwise this General Elgon would get away. And… and… the word Amritsar stopped him in his tracks. *Amritsar,* that fateful day for the British army when they fired on a crowd in the Sikh homeland in India. No. It mustn't happen here. And … he had to get Lingard back to Mbale. As they drove away he crouched on the floor of the truck carrying his fellow inspector. Blood covered the front of the European's khaki drill tunic. His face was drained of colour. The Sikh could feel the suggestion of a pulse, no more than that. He used the first aid kit to stem the flow of blood and for the rest of the journey he sat holding Lingard's hand. Well before they reached Mbale his fellow inspector was dead.

Everyone now knew General Elgon. He raised his hands. The crowd became quiet. What would happen now? Faces looked up at him as he stood on the hillock. 'I promised you power. You have that power now. And look what it has done for us. Did you not see the polisi running away? Like whipped dogs. Taking their injured. You have seen the blood. The blood of a Mzungu. This has been a victory for us, the Dini ya Mungu Wetu. If any of you had doubts forget them. We can only grow stronger.' The chant broke out. "General Elgon, General Elgon, General Elgon."

SEVENTEEN

Eight o'clock. A misty morning. Humid, a hot day ahead but cool enough at present for the men to wear collars and black ties and the women their best dresses.

The Firing party – six African policemen – aimed their rifles to the sky. Tug Wilson gave the order. 'Fire'. It was the last volley of the salute to the dead officer. Dressed in his "Number One" uniform, complete with white shirt and black tie, Sam Browne belt which glistened in the tropical sun and with blue puttees instead of the everyday long socks with blue tops, Wilson stood at the head of the grave and saluted with his sword. He nodded to the bugler. "The Last Post" echoed back from the row of eucalyptus trees which shaded the area. All of the European adult population of Mbale had attended. They now shuffled, turned and filed from the cemetery, any conversation held in low murmuring voices.

Woodley-Wills moved alongside the police commander. 'I know people are going to the Club for a sort of wake, but I don't feel ready for that. Come back to my office with me, Tug.' The policeman viewed the DC from under the peak of his cap. There was a long pause before he nodded. They walked off together.

The morning sun hadn't yet broken through the tall eucalypts to heat up the DC's office. From where he sat behind his desk Woolly Bill watched the policeman. 'Have you ever looked at the other crosses in the cemetery, Tug?' There was no reply. 'The last one was in 1927, a Forestry Officer who died from black water fever. Medicine's come a long way since then. I ...'

Wilson interrupted him. 'You don't have to make small talk for my benefit Cecil.'

'You look as though you need something.' The DC

reached down and opened the bottom drawer of his desk. He took out a bottle of Black Label whisky. 'Don't normally touch it during the day - I keep it for when any of the chiefs visit me - but I think we both might benefit from a medicinal dose.'

At first they sipped, slowly. The policeman stood up and unbuckled his Sam Browne belt and hung it up on a hook behind the door. He pointed to the ceremonial sword. 'It's only been out of its scabbard three times since I've been here – twice for Kings Birthday parades and once to cut my daughter's christening cake.' He sat down again and this time he put his head back and drained his glass. He held it out for more. 'It's so bloody quick isn't it. He was only shot yesterday but in this heat we have to bury him in twenty four hours.' The policeman paused, searching for words. They came, in a rush. 'You know, Les Lingard was a bloody good lad, only twenty-two. Dedicated to his men.' He gulped at the whisky. 'They held their own wake for him last night. Six hours of it. Some danced until they dropped. I know. I joined them. I've never thought about dancing for the dead but it seemed right somehow.' The police superintendent's voice broke. He buried his face in his hands. The DC heard a sob. This was a Tug Wilson he hadn't seen before – the hard boiled policeman who had survived Heaven knows what in Palestine. He could hear him talking even though he couldn't see his face. 'I should never have sent him up there on such a mission. I should have had better intelligence, should have gone myself.'

'You can't be everywhere, Tug. You know you had to stay here and oversee what was happening. It was one of those damned things. No one knew they had firearms.'

'I should have known, Cecil. *I* should have known.' The policeman continued to drink his whisky, more slowly now. He leant back in his chair, the front legs rising off the floor. He continued as if he had come through a barrier, 'The only consolation in this sorry business is that Gurbachan and the rest came back safely. And, of course, we know a lot more about what is happening. What we haven't talked about is Con O'Hagan.'

'Yes, Con. Father Cornelius O'Hagan …'

'I doubt if you know it but Special Branch in Kampala had him listed as an active IRA terrorist. I kept telling them not to be so stupid. He may have been once but he's been here for fifteen years. They take no notice. They regularly called for reports on his activities. Well this final report should put paid to all their nonsense once and for all. I'll get some men up there to recover his body.'

'That is what I was coming to, Tug. You've found out the hard way that they have rifles. From what Inspector Singh says there were several guns used and even if their marksmanship wasn't too good you have one dead inspector and a wounded corporal. I've been considering this since they came back. We need the army.'

'That's not on, Cecil. I can handle this without the army.'

'Look, Tug, you yourself mentioned the other day that the Police Special Force are fully occupied up in Karamoja with the cattle wars. You've no option. Good as your men are you don't have sufficient ...'

'I can't agree, Cecil, I …'

'You are the police commander for the District but I have overall responsibility and I'm going to call for the KAR.'

'I'm past arguing.' Tug raised his voice, slamming his fist on the desk. 'I will not have the army. Can't you picture what it will do to the District? We do it my way.

One of your District Officers will come as magistrate to read the Riot Act if necessary.' Wilson saw the DC's raised eyebrows. 'Oh yes, Cecil, we still have the Riot Act. So get someone to do a translation of the necessary bits into the local language. My men will recover Con O'Hagan.'

'Tug …'

'I said *my men* will recover the body'.

EIGHTEEN

To Matt Cunningham's relief Scatty Mulller had regained consciousness. Now he could carry out a thorough examination. Haltingly, and at times incoherent, his patient recounted his experience of the cave of the elephants and the millions of bats hanging from the ceiling. With what the WHO circular had said about the possible cause of the haemorrhagic fever the doctor's relief reverted to trepidation. Eventually his examination left him satisfied that it was not that disease he had so feared.

Rosemary was still in the Isolation Ward but now she knew she was no longer at risk from her contact with the road foreman. The Medical Officer focused on Scatty's leg wound. It was in a serious condition. With the uncertainty about the fever he had been able to do little about it apart from injecting antibiotics and there had been scant response to these. He took Rosemary on one side. 'Someone has got to stay with him. I've got a busy hospital to run, Sister McGregor is out at the leprosy clinic and Head Nurse Victoria is busy on the wards. Will you act as his attendant?' Uncertainty showed on her face. 'Don't worry. I'll show you how to take his temperature each half hour and how to note any changes in his condition. You can get me if you have any alarms.'

'I'll try. Will you get someone to tell Cecil? I can't think what has happened to him. I haven't seen him all the time I have been in here.'

'You don't know about Les Lingard then?'

Rosemary looked blank. 'This really is an isolation ward, you know, Matt.'

He told her what he knew about the police expedition. 'Les was shot. He was buried this morning.

It means that Cecil and Tug are busy working out what has to be done. Somehow I don't think they will see eye to eye. That's sad news to leave you with but I must get back to the wards now.'

Rosemary could see Matt's concern growing each time he returned. Late in the afternoon he took the chart she had been keeping. 'He's been getting worse throughout the day. Now his temperature is peaking more rapidly. It's septicaemia from the wound in his leg. I must go to my office. I'll be back as soon as I can.'

When he returned Cunningham's face told of his tension. 'A man less tough than Scatty would have been dead by now and he will be if we don't get him to Kampala. I've phoned for an aircraft to get him to Mulago Hospital. It's the last resort.'

'But we've no airfield here.'

'There's Tororo. It's only a short drive.'

Rosemary spread her hands out in despair. 'The last time I saw it there were lumps of stone all over it. It's half past four now. Even if they hurry it will be dark by the time the plane gets there. Tororo Rock's another thing. It's got to be several hundred feet high and it's very close to the airfield. It has to be a hazard for any night flying.'

'Tomorrow's daylight will be too late. I have asked Tug to get his inspector at Tororo to clear the airfield and to get enough cars to light the runway with their headlights. But first I must get Scatty prepared.'

'Let me know if there's anything I can do.' She left to walk back to the home she hadn't seen for three days. On her way she had to pass the District Offices. It didn't surprise her to see Cecil was still at his desk. His relief when he saw her was evident. 'Matt wouldn't stretch things and let me in to see you. I even thought about sneaking in by the back door but Victoria was on the prowl. Matt has just rung to tell me that you and Scatty have been cleared.'

'He said something about an appalling haemorrhagic fever and although we hadn't got it Scatty is very ill. Blood poisoning I believe. Did he tell you?'

'Yes. There's something you probably don't know though.'

'Go on. You sound so serious. What is it I don't know?'

'Scatty said he won't let them fly him to Kampala unless you fly with him.'

'He must be delirious. What good would that do?'

'You're being in the isolation ward has had some effect on him. He knows of the hazards at Tororo airfield and seems to think you re a lucky charm. He is aware of how ill he is. You won't be alone. Matt said Sister McGregor will go as well.'

'If Scatty's life depends upon his being treated in Kampala, I can't really say no, can I? Oh dear … that's what I said to that African on Elgon and look where it got me. I'll get some things together. Will you be OK?'

Woolly Bill was already busy with the papers on his desk.

The volcanic plug, which everyone just called "The Rock", towered nearly a thousand feet over the township of Tororo. In daylight it was visible across the whole district but when night closed in it was a flyer's nightmare. Wrapped in blankets Scatty was lying on a stretcher in the back of a police truck and exposed with him to the chilly night air was the Nursing Sister. From her seat in the front of the vehicle Rosemary peered through the windshield as they turned from the rough track onto the airfield. She could see the shapes of cars either side of the runway. A torch was signalling where the vehicle should halt.

She could just make out the local police inspector who used his torch to look at his watch. 'They've left Kampala. Someone at the police station is listening to the radio and when the plane is a quarter of an hour away he'll let us know. All the cars will turn their lights on. Daren't put them on too early in case any batteries go flat. The runway is about five hundred yards long so I've had to call in every vehicle in the area for the line up.'

The message came. The inspector gave the signal and headlights flooded the runway. Ten minutes later there was the sound of an aircraft. Rosemary looked up at the dark form of the Rock, looming over the airfield. The plane's lights appeared and she could see the aircraft now, coming lower. Lower, lower, louder. It was near the end of the runway. The Dragon Rapide aircraft started to land and then it swooped back up into the sky. She heard herself muttering, 'Oh, no, for Scatty's sake let it land.' It was circling again and this time she saw the cloud of red dust in the headlights as it made its landing. It carried on along the runway straight between the two rows of lights and came to a halt where the police truck waited. The pilot climbed down from the cockpit, the sweat on his face glistening in the cars' lights. He walked over to the tender. 'Whoever put an airfield here wants bloody shooting. On the first approach I thought I was heading straight for the Rock. Hello, I'm Chris Breen. Is the patient ready? All those headlights won't want me hanging about.' Scatty was safely loaded into the body of the plane and then Sister McGregor and Rosemary were helped up. Remembering the aborted landing Rosemary gritted her teeth and shut her eyes as the plane took off. Apart from airsickness from the bumpiness of the flight they reached hospital safely.

NINETEEN

Erinayo struggled up the last part of the steep slope to the place where the priest had been killed. He stopped and looked around recalling all too vividly the crowd when the body on the tree was uncovered. It had been obvious to him at the time that while many of the young bucks had been enthused by the sight of the Mzungu priest's degradation there was a significant number who had been disgusted by the spectacle but were too afraid of the consequences of admitting it. The shots. The police Mzungu killed. He felt confused. Had he really wanted it to go so far? Now the message had been passed up the mountain. The police were coming again and this time in greater force. He knew this could happen. It couldn't be otherwise. Now there were no crowds here. No-one baying for blood. No-one demanding the expulsion of the Wazungu. He realised he was carrying the rifle over his shoulder like the old soldier he was. It felt as though it was burning into his flesh. He had to get rid of this.

At the meeting the inner core members of the Dini Erinayo was given the task of finding Juba. He, Erinayo - who had fought in the KAR in Eritrea against the Italians and then in Burma against the Japanese - could never bring himself to call the upstart "General Elgon" like so many others did. They didn't know what war was. *General*. To them it was just a fancy name. True he had only been a rifleman but he knew, oh yes, he knew. "General Elgon" wearing a colobus monkey skin cloak. What pretention. The Dini must now quietly fade away – it could always be resurrected later if the time seemed right. He arrived at the cave by the fig tree. He smelt a cooking fire's smoke. There would be someone there. It had to be the *General* himself.

The man he was seeking must have heard him and appeared from the cave. 'Erinayo. What do you want?'

Erinayo was affronted. No greetings. It was the worst of bad manners. It was an unbreakable custom not to use the time-honoured greetings. 'I want to talk to you Juba.'

'Why?'

'I have met with the others. We talked about what happened when the polisi came. It is true we beat them. But what comes next? … I will tell you. They are coming again. More of them. The will send their Special Force. Hard men from the North. Tear gas. More rifles. And if by chance we beat them again then it will be the army.'

'You are laying out excuses because you are cowards. If we don't take our chance now it will never come again.'

'Get your head out of the clouds. Look at what really happened. We killed a Muzungu polisi but that was not good shooting. It was luck.'

'You always boasted you were a KAR and were a good shot. And that you could train the others to be as good as you.'

'I thought that because some are good hunters they would make riflemen but it was hard enough trying to get them to hold the rifles properly. And we needed more ammunition. As for me, I am finding that my eyesight isn't what it was during the war …

'More excuses. No wonder no-one wanted you to lead the Dini…'

'That may be so, but I've been chosen to come and tell you that the Dini is no longer active. What's more, I have to tell you that you have to go. Leave Elgon. All you have done is bring us trouble.'

'I will go if I choose to.'

'If you don't go, they will kill you. You're not really

108

one of us. We are not afraid to do that. The polisi blame you for the death of their Muzungu and will give a reward. You must do what you want. I will leave you now.' Erinayo started to walk away and then he stopped, took the rifle from his shoulder and handed it to Juba. 'Take this. I don't want it any more.' He took the track that would lead back to his village but he had no intention of leaving the area. When he knew he was out of sight of the cave he climbed a hill from where he could look out over the clearing. After a time he saw Juba emerge from the cave but he was not alone. A man who he had never seen before followed, so tall he had to bow his head to avoid hitting the lip of the cave's opening. Juba was carrying a long bundle and the other man had a bedding roll slung from his shoulder. That was enough for Erinayo. The general was going, really going. He resumed his journey to his village. He had to hurry. He needed help for what he had to do before the polisi arrived.

Juba and his companion took a track which led higher up the mountain. They carried on walking without speaking until they reached the start of the giant sorrel. They sat in the crevice of a rock from where they had a good field of vision. 'You heard what that hyena had to say, Fulani?'

The Kenyan nodded. 'What did you expect? You were never going to persuade enough people to join the Dini. If we succeed in Kenya things will be different here. We could do with you, you are wasting your talents here.'

'You too think I should leave Elgon?'

'Yes. You can't stay here now. Someone will inform on you and the polisi will arrest you. We need someone in Kampala. We have a house there you can use. But first we need money. I had to leave in a hurry and I've got nothing now.'

'I know where we can get some.'

Rosemary received hardly any letters from England and so she was surprised to find one addressed to her when she went to collect mail from their Post Office box. The handwriting was vaguely familiar and yet she couldn't place it. She was tempted to open it on the spot but she waited until she returned home. It really was a voice from the past:

Dear Rosemary

At last I've got round to writing to you. I was in Oxford recently so I went to the farm and got your address. Your folk weren't very welcoming – I'm sure it's because they think it was me who steered you towards Cecil and therefore on to Africa rather than staying to labour with them at the farm. Your Dad still thinks you would have made a good Land Girl. Did he have any of those during the war?

Anyway, I'm prattling on. When we were at the Secretarial College we said we would always keep in touch. We haven't been very good at it have we? So let me bring you up to date. I stayed on working at the College Library for quite a time after you left but In 1944 one of the profs. Persuaded me to apply for a secretarial post – guess where – Buckingham Palace no less. I found out later that he had connections in Whitehall and he had been asked to find someone "who could be trusted". Wheels within wheels, that's how these things work I guess. Doesn't pay all that well but there are some perks.

So I've been here ever since. I came after the air raids but the King and Queen stayed here all the way through the war. It's been a nerve-wracking time. I don't think I'm breaking the Official Secrets Act when I say that HM's health has not been very good for some time. He still took on duties – like opening the Festival of Britain – when he should have been taking it easier. At least he didn't do the Trooping of the Colour this year. Princess Elizabeth did it instead, riding a horse called Winston. And now he's had an operation. That was quite a business. They went to great lengths say some of the other staff to create a full scale operating theatre in the Palace.

The King and Queen were due to do a tour of parts of the Commonwealth but because of the health problems Princess Elizabeth and the Duke of Edinburgh are going to do this instead. And do you know – and this is what prompted me to write to you just now – they are going to stay a short time in Kenya on their way to Australia. The people of Kenya gave them a lodge somewhere out in the back of beyond as a wedding present and it's said that's where they are going to stay.

Now the even more exciting part. Would you believe I've been asked to go with the Royal Party. Only a minor role, naturally, and of course I shan't travel on the same plane as them. It will be the first time I've flown. What's the chance of us being able to meet up? I'll write to you again when I know more about the details.

They were good times in Oxford weren't they. Fancy, though, you married Sanders of the River and me working in Buck House. By the way, you've always known me as Liz. At work I'm Betty. Puzzled? There might be one too many Elizabeths around!!!

All the very best from your old friend

I'm sure I'm still Liz to you

Rosemary smiled as she finished reading. It would be lovely to see Liz again but wondered if she knew what it was like travelling in East Africa. Nairobi wasn't just down the road and that was where she was likely to be.

Tug Wilson knew he had spent too long in conflict with the DC but now he and his men were on their way and he was exhilarated and uncomfortable at the same time. Exhilarated because of the action that was coming and the chance to bring in the killers of Inspector Lingard and Con O'Hagan; uncomfortable because he could feel his relationship with Cecil Woodley-Wills changing. He liked Woolly Bill, respected him, his straight talking and deep experience of Uganda. If there was any European who had a better understanding of the complexities of the people of this country he was yet to meet him. He would hate to lose his comradeship. There was patching up to be done. He would have to find time for that later.

It was mid-day before the police arrived at the burnt out offices of the chief. An unseen goat bleated. There was the smell of cooking fires but there was no sign of people. Gurbachan took a squad and searched the area around the clearing. 'There's no-one to be found, Sir. They heard us coming and ran away. Even those who haven't been involved will be scared. We've found the priest's motor cycle - burned out.'

'There's no point in anyone staying here. We must find O'Hagan's body and then look for this man they call "General Elgon". We will go on foot.' They followed the track that Gurbachan knew only too well, the track where Lingard had died as they bumped their way down in the vehicle. They worked their way higher up the mountain. It was neither a climb nor a walk. The

112

gradient became steeper and at times they were forced to clamber over rocky outcrops, gasping for breath as the air became thinner. They reached the saucer shaped clearing. This was where Lingard was unlucky enough to be hit by the ricochet.

Wilson could now see the fig tree. He beckoned for Gurbachan Singh to join him. 'Is that where you saw the priest's body? I can't see anything now.'

'It was there. I saw it. Someone must have removed it.' said the inspector. As they talked a man emerged from the cave. The quiet was broken by the sound of the policemen working rifle bolts. The man started walking towards them, spreading out his arms to show he had no weapons. He spoke in Swahili. 'I am Erinayo. I am the Chief of this area. If you don't believe me ask the DC.' He stopped and looked around as if searching for Woodley-Wills.

'Keep walking towards us, slowly,' commanded Wilson. The man kept coming. A decoy? Someone to divert their attention? His Palestine experiences flooded his mind. Both Jews and Arabs had been expert at these tactics. 'What are you doing here?'

The man was unkempt, hardly looking like a chief but he had authority in his manner. 'I knew the polisi would come. I have been waiting here for you since that terrible day.'

'What terrible day?'

'The day when the Muzungu polisi was killed.'

'Where are all the other people who were here?'

'They have gone back to their homes. They didn't like what happened. They want no part of the Dini.'

'You were here when the Inspector was shot?'

'Yes, but I only came because we would be punished if we didn't come.'

'Did you see who fired at the police?'

'No. They were hidden in the trees.' The longer

113

Erinayo talked the more they knew he had been involved but there was no evidence to connect him with the shootings. Eventually the Chief said, 'There is something for you.' Cautiously they followed him across the clearing. He disappeared into the cave and reappeared dragging a long bundle wrapped in bark cloth. There could be no doubt it was a body. 'You should take it. He must have a burial according to the customs of his people.'

Wilson loosened the fibre with which it was wound and opened an end of the bundle. He could see the head of a European. With the damage caused by birds and animals it was hard to identify his features. What was left of the hair was the right colour. There was no-one else it could be but Father O'Hagan. He turned to Erinayo. 'What else have you got in here?'

'It is not my cave Effendi. Juba was using it. I do not know what he kept here.'

A search of the cave found eleven rifles hidden under brushwood. A wooden box held a few rounds of ammunition. At first by torchlight the rifles looked like sporting weapons but then Wilson realised they were Lee Enfields with the wood work cut down. He had heard rumour of the theft from the Police Armoury in Kampala. These had to be the stolen weapons. The sense of elation was growing again but the only way he was going to clear up this mess was by getting the man they called "General Elgon".

Wilson spent two days in the area. Enquiries were made. Stories conflicted, were muddled and packed with hearsay evidence but little came to light that would take him further forward other than a rich seam that could undoubtedly convict "General Elgon" – or Juba Wanyama as he now knew him. He returned to Mbale satisfied that the "Dini" was no longer active and that once more there seemed to be peace in the area.

TWENTY

THE UGANDA HERALD

Kampala: Monday 8th October.1951

On Sunday night, robbers attacked the house of Mr. Ashabhai Patel, the owner and manager of Magodes Ginnery, which is between Mbale and Tororo. Mr Patel told our reporter that Mr. Tarlokh Singh Moli, the ginnery's engineer, confronted the robbers with his sword but during the struggle was shot dead. Later the body of the African night-watchman was found in the ginnery compound. He had been stabbed.

Mr. Patel further told our reporter that two robbers entered his house around midnight but there could have been more outside that he did not see. They escaped with a large sum of money in the ginnery's pick up truck. He praised Mr. Singh's courage in tackling the robbers. "I would not be talking to you now if he had not wielded his sword," said the ginery owner.

The Bugishu District Police commander, Superintendent Stanley Wilson told us that he is leading the investingation assisted by Inspector Gurbachan Singh. He has every confidence that the people responsible will be apprehended. However, it is too soon for any more detailed information to be made public.

The invitation had been for seven o'clock but it was well past eight when Tug Wilson and his wife Maureen arrived at the Woodley-Wills' for dinner.

'Sorry we're late, Cecil. I'm sure you know why.'

'That business at Magodes?'

'What else.'

'Well, I'm sure a Bell beer straight from the fridge and Rosemary's cooking will put it at the back of your mind for an hour or two.' The pre-dinner conversation stayed on domestic matters. It was a time honoured custom there should be no talk about work.

'How is the old woman from Elgon getting on, Rosemary?' Maureen Wilson had never met Flora. 'There seems to be a lot of mystery about her. I'm surprised she has stayed with you. What's her name?'

'Flora. She's a marvel. She's making three or four statuettes every week now – and selling them through The CMS Bookshop. She feels so strongly about my helping her that she's even keeping me in pin money. It's like she's one of the family.' Rosemary caught Woolly Bill's grimace. It wasn't long before the conversation flagged. Tug's silence was beginning to tell on the others. Rosemary was particularly uncomfortable; normally he was flatteringly attentive. 'Let's go through to dinner. I picked up my Kenya meat basket from the train at Tororo this morning so the beef isn't going to be like boot leather. I've done Beef Wellington in your honour,' and with this ushered her guests to the dining room'.

They were half way through the meal and Tug hadn't said a word. Cecil poured the policeman another glass of beer. 'You can't keep it all to yourself, Tug, the raid on the ginnery and the killings must be on your mind. Why don't you tell us about them?'

Wilson toyed a little with his food and at last put his fork down. 'OK. I'll tell you the little I know. Ashabhai

116

had drawn money for paying his staff plus more for other running expenses. It was a tidy sum – five thousand three hundred shillings he said. He and his family had gone to bed and it was well into the night when he heard noises. He lit a lantern and went into his living room. Two men were trying the door of his safe – well it's not really a safe, just a big enamelled cash box bolted into the wall. They threatened him with a panga. They said they would dismember his wife and children if he didn't produce the money. He was certain they were in earnest and so he unlocked the cash box and handed over the money. Then his chief mechanic, Tarlokh Singh appeared. He was waving a sword and swung at one of the men, missed him and the other one shot him. They demanded the key for the ginnery's truck and made off in it.'

'Could he recognise them again?'

'Ashabhai says he might be able to but his wife was peeping round the door and she is certain she could identify one of them. She said the lantern clearly lit up the face of the one who was doing all the talking.'

The room was quiet once more as they ate dessert. Woolly Bill led the way through to the lounge and for coffee. Once the cups had been handed round he said, 'So where do you go from here, Tug?'

'Can't this wait until tomorrow in the office, Cecil?'

'Up to you, but you'd be better company if you'd say something.'

'That's what's got me. It's two days since it happened and we know nothing more than I have just told you. In a case of murder if you don't make progress in the first forty-eight hours you generally don't crack it at all. Nearly all the homicides here are African on African beer party or grudge killings and apart from making sure the file will stand up in the High Court there's no difficulty with these. I had the

Commissioner on the phone this afternoon wanting to know when an arrest would be made. The only victim he seemed concerned about was the Asian who is prominent in his community. No-one rings up from HQ when it's an African murder.'

'Is there nothing more to go on, Tug,' asked Rosemary.

'Matt carried out a post mortem on Mr. Moli. He found the bullet that killed him. .38 - that must have come from a revolver. Apart from that, not a damn thing. I've got good detectives – they don't come better than my Detective Sergeant. Speaks seven or eight languages which means he can get informers in all sorts of places. Not one of these can tell him anything. We lifted some fragmentary fingerprints but the day hasn't come when we can go through the thousands on file at HQ and make comparisons. They'll only come in handy after an arrest.'

Rosemary persisted. 'What about the vehicle they took?'

'Probably driven into a swamp. The money is in old notes. Unless they flash it around at a beer party we won't find it. The long and short of it is I haven't any idea who did it. Local? Probably. There's a chance it might be incomers who had some inside information. Ashabhai collects the money the same time each month.'

'I've got a thought, Tug. Promise me you won't laugh.' The policeman smiled – the first time that evening. 'You say Ashabhai *might* be able to identify one of them and his wife says she is sure she can. I've read of identity parades in crime novels. What is an identity parade?'

'When, *when*, you've got a suspect you get together ten or so people who are about the same age, height and similar appearance. The suspect stands where he likes in a line up and if the witness recognises anyone he points that person out. There are some legal niceties but that's the essence of it. But we haven't got a suspect so why are you interested in identity parades?'

'I have a hunch … if we had a line up of some of Flora's statuettes and that of a man *I suspect* was included would that do as an identity parade for Mr and Mrs Ashabhai?

'That's ridiculous Rosemary…'

'Don't look at me as though I'm crazy Cecil … couldn't it be worth doing Tug? You've seen how life-like her sculptures are. If it worked you'd at least know what one of them looked like.'

The policeman sat shaking his head. 'What makes you think you have a good suspect?'

'I told you. I have a hunch and my hunches are pretty good. Aren't they, Cecil? Go on, Tug, humour me. What have you got to lose?'

Woolly Bill surprised his wife. 'I don't know where she gets these ideas but it's hair brained enough to make it interesting. I'll go along with it, only because it's made me curious.'

Rosemary beamed. 'Well thank you Cecil. I didn't expect such a fulsome vote of confidence.'

'Well, that's it then. You've hooked me. Tomorrow morning eight a.m. at the Police Station then Rosemary. With all the identity parade members. If I like the look of it in the flesh – well you know what I mean, in the clay I suppose – we'll get Ashabhai and his wife to come in. And now I think it's time for bed. Are you ready, Maureen?'

As they walked the short distance to their house Maureen said, 'That's the new Rosemary for you. Something's happened to that girl. I'd love to know what she'll do next.'

TWENTY-ONE

Rosemary was up at her usual early hour but instead of watching the dawn from her verandah she dressed and spent the next hour with Flora who would only agree to the statuettes being taken to the police station if she could come and watch how they were used. The "suspect" was the model of the man Rosemary met on Elgon. Why did she pick him? She realised she had no good reason for this other than his appearance still made her shudder as she thought what would have happened if Scatty had been infected with the virus. And that was no reason at all to connect him with the ginnery robbery. She thought of calling the whole thing off but she'd gone too far now to do this. Together Rosemary and the old woman packed eleven statuettes in her estate car. As she set them out on the desk in Wilson's office she checked with the policeman. 'What do you think? Do we go ahead?'

Tug Wilson stood back and surveyed the line up. 'I'm amazed. They're so life-like I feel I could talk with them. We're on, Rosemary. Let's do it.'

'That's what I wanted to hear. I've written down where the suspect is standing. I'm not going to tell you which he is.'

'I'll send for Ashabhai and his wife.'

While Flora stood quietly in the corner of the room Rosemary sat by the desk nursing her apprehensions. Was she going to be the laughing stock of Mbale? Such things got around like a bush fire. She heard a car arrive. It was the Patels. She watched Tug taking them into another room. At last she heard Ashabhai talking as the policeman brought him along the verandah to the office. His voice was raised.

'Mr. Wilson, this is folly. I thought you had the

120

robbers. You are making a fool of me asking me to identify clay figures.' Rosemary heard mumbled voices then Ashabhai raised his voice, 'If I must, let's get on with it.' They stopped outside the door. There was the final briefing and they came into the room. Ashabhai walked slowly along the line, and then he bent forward to take a closer look. He went back to the beginning of the line and started again. He put his hand out tentatively towards the statuette of Juba and pulled it away quickly. 'I think... no, I'm not sure. Gracious me that one stares like him, but no I cannot say it was him.'

When Ashabhai had left the room Rosemary rearranged the figurines with Juba in a different position. All the while Flora watched attentively. Gurbachan Singh brought Mrs. Patel into the room. She shuffled along the line, turned and shuffled back even more diffidently. *That's it then, how am I going to live this down.* Then Mrs. Patel stretched out her hand and placed it on the head of the statuette of Juba. She spoke quietly to Gurbachan in Hindi.

'She says that is the man who threatened her husband. She has no doubt whatever. She is one hundred per cent sure.' Rosemary saw Flora nodding her head.

The clay figures had been packed away and Tug had reclaimed his office. 'How on earth did you pick that one out of all the rest?'

'I really don't know, Tug. Somehow it just seemed right.'

'Well, now we have a good idea of what one of them looks like. I'll have to see how this will take us forward.'

Rosemary thought for a moment. 'I've got my camera in the car. I'm going to take a close up photo and get some posters made at the print shop. We can send these out around the District.'

'Slow down, Rosemary. Get a photo but first I'll show it to Inspector Singh and Detective Oboran. If we're lucky they might know who he is.' She took photos from several angles, the local photographer developed them and she brought them back to the police station the following day. Tug Wilson summoned Gurbachan and Oboran. The Detective shook his head. 'No-one I know. I can show the photos around.' Gurbachan had stood quietly while the detective had viewed the pictures. Wilson turned to him. Gurbachan smiled. 'It just happens I know this man.'

'Go on,' Wilson urged him. 'Who is it?'

'It is the man who was responsible for the death of the Catholic priest. He was known as "General Elgon" but his name is really Juba Wanyama. He was there inciting the crowd when Inspector Lingard was shot.'

'All we've got to do is find him,' said the Superintendent. The Inspector smiled, a rueful smile. He thought of that fateful day on Elgon and the visit to Muller's camp. And Lingard, buried and gone. It's just what he said then - *"Now we've got to find him."*

In a house rented by a Kenya man in Nyangole village bordering Tororo station Juba and Fulani crouched talking to a constable from the local police station. He was showing them one of the photographs that had been circulated from Mbale. While he was still running the Railway tea stall Fulani had kept the constable sweet with occasional handouts as an insurance policy. Now the chickens were coming home to roost. 'This is worth some more shillings. Keep in touch.' After the constable had gone he held the photo up and compared it with Juba. 'That old witch is still spinning her magic. This is too good a likeness. You'll have to stay here until you can grow a beard and longer hair. Then we'll catch a night train to Kampala.'

'Why? I don't know anyone in Kampala…'

Fulani cut him short. 'We have work for you there and somewhere for you to live.' The Kenyan carried on, 'I know your habits - this time when you travel you'll pay the fare.' They laughed a little louder than the joke warranted.

Juba's hair now hung down in dreadlocks and his lower face was covered with a beard. They caught the Mail Train from the next station up line from Tororo. No more than a crossing place for trains there were few people there and no-one who would know either of them. To Juba the journey seemed to take for ever. They bought food at Jinja and at last the train pulled into a minor station, five miles outside Kampala, nine hours after their journey had started. One of the many overloaded illegal taxis took them to the market at Katwe, a suburb of Kampala.

They threaded their way between a cluster of small houses, each surrounded by a patch of cooking banana trees. Fulani pointed to one. He unlocked the padlock securing the door. 'This is one of ours. You will be safe here – if you use your common sense. When it's dark bury that thing you are carrying in your bedding roll. We don't know who will be nosing around. I will keep in touch.'

Juba felt strange in this urban setting but he accepted that it was a melting pot of tribes, people who had moved into the growing city, townsmen in the making, and an ideal place for someone like him to lose himself from the eyes of authority. Fulani introduced him to the work that would pay for his keep, and more –sending cannabis by railway to the coast from where it was shipped to Arabia. As he became familiar with the area he began to feel secure. Despite this – or perhaps because of it – he was restless. He missed the mountain's clear air but more than that he missed the cut and thrust for leadership that the Dini ya Mungu Wetu gave him and the power he could wield there. Here he was just another countryman sucked into the city.

The Kenyan organisation was treating him well but when and in what way would they want their pay off from him?

TWENTY-TWO

Mbale had been rocked by the events. The Asian population was still shocked by the death of Tarlokh Singh even though a month had passed since the robbery at the ginnery and in Mbale Club - the place where most Europeans met - hushed voices recalled what Les Lingard had contributed to the life of the station. They had not recovered from his murder and a sense of vulnerability accompanied this. Every creak of the corrugated iron of the roof at night, every unrecognised African in the servants' quarters, every unfamiliar vehicle passing along the roads where the government bungalows were located brought a reaction that was never there before.

Tug Wilson was frustrated at his lack of progress in making an arrest even though now, thanks to Rosemary's initiative, he had a strong suspect.

Rosemary continued to nurture Flora's work and gained contentment from this until Cecil dropped the bombshell in her lap as she sat reading before going to bed. 'The new Governor is having a shake-up. The Chief Secretary phoned me this afternoon. H.E. wants me in one of the Ministries in Entebbe.'

'Why? We haven't been here all that long. Haven't you always said you're a District man?'

'H.E. wants me to start work on framing the Constitution for the country when it becomes independent. He seems to think I am the right man for the job.'

'Independence? I thought you said that was thirty years off.'

'It will come sooner than most think. The Americans and Russians are pushing us hard.'

'Entebbe; I hate the place. I can't see me fitting in

125

there. I don't want to go. Can't you just say no?'

'My dear, I can't refuse… it has come straight from H.E himself. I know I have turned down going there in the past but this if different. As a matter of fact I like the man. He's got something that previous Governors didn't have. It's not as though you won't know anyone. There'll be several of the wives you have known in the past. You'll soon settle in.'

'Oh yes, a host of coffee mornings. How soon have you got to be there?'

'Right away. We'll have to start packing as soon as possible.'

'What about Flora?'

'What about her? She's not really our responsibility.'

'I think she is, Cecil. She comes with us… assuming she will want to.'

'For Heavens sake, Rosemary, we can't do that…'

'Why not? Flora comes, or I stay here. I'm sure someone will give me board and lodging.' She said no more, closed her book and went through to bed.

Three weeks later the Woodley-Wills were moving into their allocated house in Entebbe near the shore of Lake Victoria. Cecil started work in earnest as soon as they arrived leaving the house early in the morning and not returning until late in the evening. Rosemary felt she was regressing. There weren't even the minor duties – Cecil's left-overs – that she had in Mbale. She could do with Mrs. Khan's wisdom once more.

She had seen little of Flora, who was obviously unsettled by the move. The old woman had taken to leaving her quarters early in the morning and not returning until late at night. At first this puzzled Rosemary but then it dawned on her that she had no clay and had no idea where to get it. Entebbe housed the Government Geology Department and it wasn't long before she found her way to a supply of clay as good as she had found on Elgon. Flora resumed her sculpting. Now she was producing images of local people, so different from her earlier work. She joined the small group of Wakamba wood carvers outside the Lake Victoria Hotel who sold their work from under a large fig tree close to the hotel's patio.

Rosemary began promoting Flora through posters and pamphlets in the airport and hotel. Soon tourists and aircrew were asking for Flora by name and she could hardly manage to keep up with the demand. Her fame spread. First a U.K. national newspaper ran a feature article about her and this was followed by a spread in a magazine in the U.S.A.

Rosemary no longer had time to brood on her own concerns. As Flora's business manager she had little time to call her own. Packing the busts and statuettes for export, mother-henning the old woman at a stream of interviews and looking after her accounts demanded all her energy. Flora's bank balance grew at an astonishing rate.

She now had a role that gave her pride. She saw more of Flora than she did of Cecil. Though he hardly noticed this.

TWENTY-THREE

'Is the P.M. available?' He recognised the King's physician's voice. The anxiety was obvious.

'No. He's in a meeting with the Foreign Minister. I could pass a message if it's urgent.'

'It's urgent and it's important. Tell him the King insists he is going to go to the airport tomorrow. I have tried to persuade him that he's not strong enough yet but he is determined to go. There is no telling what the outcome will be.'

'I'll tell him as soon as I can, though I doubt Winston will have any more success than you.'

In September the King's right lung was removed in an operation at Buckingham Palace. Since then he had still not been seen in public and his commitments were taken up by others. He had entrusted the most important of these to his daughter Elizabeth. Believing that the preservation of the Commonwealth required that the royal visit to Australasia must go ahead it had been arranged that the Princess and her husband would undertake it in his stead. The royal couple were to fly to Kenya, take a short holiday there and then sail on from Mombasa in the liner S.S. Gothic for the rest of their 30,000 miles tour of Commonwealth countries. If he could not make the Royal Tour himself the very least he could do he was to make sure he went to the airport to see his daughter's departure.

It was the 31st January 1952, a miserable winter's day. No-one had been able to dissuade the King. And now as he stood waiting even the thick Ulster overcoat could not keep the cold and damp from chilling right through to the marrow of his bones. His party watched from the viewing gallery as Captain Parker prepared the Argonaut aircraft G-ALHK "Atlanta" for take-off.

Soon it was lost in the leaden winter skies over West London. Without a word, the King turned and started to walk back into the airport building.

Princess Elizabeth and her husband flew direct to the RAF station of El Adem in Libya where "Atlanta" was refuelled. They flew on to Kenya and once the landing formalities were complete they headed for the fishing lodge at Sangana in the foothills of Mount Kenya, a gift from the Kenyan people on their marriage in 1947.

Twenty miles from Sangana was a waterhole which attracted game of all kinds, from the smallest antelope to elephants and lions. Years earlier the owner of the land, Eric Walker, decided to build a tree house with viewing deck and observation rooms overlooking the waterhole and it wasn't a big step to make this into a small hotel which became known as "Treetops". Walker invited the royal couple to stay there. The Princess - a very keen photographer - was keen to take cine films under the watchful eye of the resident hunter, Jim Corbet. On February 6th she went to bed high above the ground in one of "Treetops" cabin-like rooms. The following day, after watching rhinos fighting near the waterhole she and her husband returned to Sangana Lodge.

At his Sandringham Estate on 5th February the King had returned from a shooting party, had dined and retired to bed. The following morning his valet, James McDonald, ran his bath. The King was normally awakened by this activity but that morning the lack of movement worried the valet who summoned a doctor. George VI had died in his sleep.

Now the Princess had to be told. The isolation of Sangana Lodge made contact difficult and it wasn't until that afternoon that the news reached the Duke of Edinburgh's private secretary. The Duke decided to tell his wife of the death of her father as they walked in the gardens of the lodge. Jim Corbet noted the occasion with his entry in "Treetops" visiting book – "*For the first time in the history of the world a young girl climbed into a tree one day a Princess and after having what she described as her most thrilling experience she climbed down from the tree the next day a Queen*".

Now the authorities were faced with the task of returning the new Queen to the United Kingdom as quickly as possible. Even to travel to Nairobi would have added too many hours to the journey. A Dakota aircraft was sent to Nanyuki, the nearest airfield to Sangana, to fly to Entebbe where the Argonaut would be waiting for the onward journey to England.

TWENTY-FOUR

Juba was not a superstitious man. Even so, the dry storms with forked lightning bouncing around Kampala's many hill tops made him uneasy. When he was a small boy he had listened as the older people had filled the evening air with talk. They played games with their words, using time-honoured proverbs to add colour to their banter. One of these aphorisms was dragged deep from his memory now by the shafts of aerial bombardment. *"Lightning without rain is the devil throwing his spears."* The consequence of this they all knew was the creation of bottomless pits, down which goats and humans disappeared, a portent of disaster to come. Of course he didn't believe any of this – these were only old peoples' word games on the same level as the ideas that the missionaries had force-fed him. He sat by the door of his house absorbed as much in his memories as in watching the display. It would be even more spectacular when night fell.

Fulani shook his shoulder. 'You want to be more careful.' Juba hadn't seen the Kenyan arrive. 'I might have been the polisi looking for you. Aren't you going to greet me? You Uganda people spend ages on your greetings and you don't mean half of what you say.'

'I won't waste my breath then. In any case I'm not one of those Uganda people. Why have you come here? The polisi want you as much as me.'

'I have a message for you from Nairobi. It is too important to wait.'

'I haven't seen you in months and now you come telling me something is urgent.' The Kenyan moved his head close to Juba's and whispered into his ear. Juba stiffened. 'Is this a joke? How can you know all this?'

'We have people in places you would never guess.

That is how we know. You, man of Uganda, have been chosen. You have been given big responsibility now. There are people in Nairobi – important people – who will be waiting for you to achieve this. You still want our people to support you don't you?'

'Of course that's what I want. We've talked about it you and me so many times.'

'Then you've no time to waste. You've still got it?'

'I'm not likely to get rid of something like that am I?'

'There's a taxi in Katwe Market driven by a man they call Nyoka.' Juba raised his eyebrows at the name. 'Yes Nyoka. You'll see why when you meet him. He's been told you are coming. He knows he has to get you there as fast as he can.'

'I know it's an honour to do this but why hasn't one of your people been chosen? Why not you? You're here.'

'It's obvious. You know your way around this place better than any of us. We're wasting time talking. Go and get ready. I shall leave now. It's better we are not seen together.' It was beginning to get dark as Fulani slipped away.

Juba took his hoe. He walked slowly round to the garden at the back of his house watching for any nearby movement as he went. The patch was shielded by a stretch of bamboo matting and some banana trees. Even though the visibility was poor he again looked around cautiously before he started digging. He knelt and ran his fingers through the earth, groping and feeling. At last he felt the hardness of the gun through the cloth that wrapped it. He lifted the bundle from the hole and ripped off the covering. He concealed it in a roll of bedding. Then he measured three lengths of his hoe in the direction of the nearest banana plant and dug again. He fell to his knees and sifted the earth through his fingers. He sifted again. Nothing. Time was racing away but this next item was vital. His fingers were shaking when he pulled the small packet from the earth. He slipped it into his pocket. Now he was ready.

He had to get to Katwe market quickly. He slung the bedding roll over his shoulder and walked slowly past the bar that served his area. His luck was in. He saw the bicycle leaning against the outside wall. He was now chancing being spotted and risking the alarm being raised. If it was, he would be chased, caught and beaten to death. It was a risk he had to take.

The luck still held; he arrived at the market safely. The place was teeming with people. He must find Nyoka and his taxi. Bars and eating places ringed the market place and the crowds were thickest round these, catching up on last minute snacks before boarding the taxis. These were all unlicensed, Peugeot estate cars with metal luggage racks welded to their roofs and running the length of the vehicle. Despite their illegality they were faster and more reliable than the buses. Even though they waited for their passengers close to Katwe Police Station action was never taken against any of them. Unless, of course, they failed to pay the Traffic police with their shining white crash helmets and sparkling new BSA Golden Flash motor cycles.

Always so much in control of himself, Juba for once felt panic. Fulani had given him no programme of the events to take place that evening. 'Just get there as soon as you can,' he had said. 'You'll know soon enough whether you are in time.' And what did that mean? 'It means I have got to find Nyoka quickly,' he muttered to himself. He hitched his bedding roll higher on his shoulder and went to the first taxi he could see. 'Iko Wapi Taxi ya Nyoka?' he asked in the common language of Swahili.

133

The taxi driver looked at Juba disdainfully. 'I am Muganda. I do not speak Swahili.' He felt his anger rising. Why was everyone trying to slow him down? He tried again in English. This time the taxi driver nodded and pointed with his chin. 'Over there, at the end of the row.' Juba elbowed his way through the throng until he was near enough to speak to the driver. The estate car was already crammed with people and the roof rack was overflowing with bedding and huge bunches of cooking bananas. There was no need to ask if he was "Nyoka". Nyoka. Swahili for snake. The man's head craned forward, swaying slightly. His tongue flicking between his teeth.

It was obvious he was not a Muganda so Juba spoke again in Swahili. 'I was told by Fulani to take your taxi.' The answer came in Juba's father's language. 'I've been waiting for you. These people are getting impatient. I am lucky not to lose them to other taxis. Put that bedding up on the roof and get in here.' Nyoka pointed to the passenger seat.

'My bedding comes inside with me.'

'Please yourself. It will be uncomfortable for you. And it will cost you five shillings more.' Juba's hand bunched into a fist but this was no time for arguing. The door creaked as he pulled it open and his stiff load jammed painfully into his side as he climbed into the vehicle. Nyoka was holding his hand out. 'I know where you are going. Just pay me.' He was still speaking in the Kenyan language. Juba found his money with difficulty while the other passengers jeered. If they knew what he was about to do they wouldn't bray like that. Finally he managed to place the note and coins in the driver's hand.

There was not much traffic on the road and all the passengers were going beyond Juba's destination. The taxi slowed as it reached the outskirts of the Township.

It stopped at the unofficial taxi park by the quay where the Lake steamers discharged their passengers. They passed the Lake Victoria Hotel, a beacon of light in the dark, guests sitting drinking on the flag stoned forecourt. Now there was only the road which led out of the Township and past the airport, which, even though it had but one runway and very limited facilities, had just that year been classified as "International". As they passed the airport Juba craned his neck to get a good a view of the buildings and the apron in front of them. There was the big plane, parked a short distance away from the buildings. He held back the cry of relief. A plane that big must be hers. Perhaps she hadn't gone yet.

The driver stopped when they had travelled a quarter of a mile or so beyond the airport and in the dark Juba eased himself from the Peugeot, hauling his bedding roll out as quietly as he could. Nyoka spoke in their language. 'Do you know where I will be later tonight? The taxi park near where the boats come in. I shan't wait all night.' Before Juba could gather his thoughts the solitary flickering rear light of the taxi disappeared into the darkness.

He picked his way through the elephant grass that bordered the road. He knew that the runway went all the way from where he was standing almost to the shore of Lake Victoria. He had to cross the tarmac as soon as possible to be near the big plane but he couldn't risk doing so too near the buildings.

How much time did he have? He had no idea. He could see strands of wire reflecting the building's lights. He felt his way forward until he could lean and touch them. The perimeter fence; now he must follow this towards the Lake. No-one could see him from the other side now. But there were other hazards. Hippos left the Lake at night time to graze. Anger one of those and that would be the end of him. Crocodiles, too, crawled onto the land to lie in the long grass. The thought of these creatures sharpened Juba's senses.

He was far enough away from the buildings. The fence - four strands of wire on posts - was no more than a marker for the perimeter of the airport. It was easier than he thought. He climbed through the fence. The noise of the rifle touching the wire sent him sprawling onto the ground. He looked across the runway to the airport building. Nothing moved. He climbed slowly to his feet and continued towards the lake. He turned and started to cross the runway. Still no reaction from the buildings.

He was across; no sentries patrolling. How stupid these people are. Now he had to work his way back towards the buildings. Stupid they may be but he must still keep his senses working. Maybe they had laid a trap for him - betrayed by the Kenya man. Ridiculous. Why should he think that? He pulled some caked cannabis from his pocket and chewed on it. This would help him; keep his nerves in order.

Keeping close to the fence he moved slowly towards the airport buildings. The apron was lit by lights mounted high on the control tower but there was no lighting close to the side of the building. It was going to be easier than he expected. He could see people moving inside. A Muzungu police officer was talking to other Wazungu but there was no sign of his target. He was in a good position close to a brick outhouse. Out of the light but with a clear line of fire all the way from the airport doors to the moveable steps to the aircraft.

Then he heard the sound in the distance. An aircraft, coming from the direction of the Lake. He crouched as he could hear it flying closer. Its lights were flickering. Closer. Noisier. Now screeching. Right overhead. Brilliant landing lights showing up the runway and momentarily blinding him. The stench of aviation fuel.

But the big plane had to be hers. It was already here. Could it be soldiers flying in? He flung himself flat. He watched as the plane – two engines with propellers whirling – bounced slightly on the tarmac, puffs of smoke coming from the tyres. It had landed. He lay as still as he could, raising his head enough to watch the plane as it turned and taxied from the end of the runway towards the building. He could see the steps being wheeled towards it. The door of the aircraft opened. He was still lying on his stomach and he had to crane his neck to see who would come out. A man. No uniform. So far so good.

He still kept down. But now there was a woman at the plane's door. He could see her clearly in the powerful lights. Was it really her? No-one that young could be a queen. Could he get to his feet in time? Before he could try the man moved in front of her as they went down the steps. He could only see her head. Just as well. He must be absolutely sure it was the right person.

They had all left the plane by now. Of course it must be her. There was no other woman present. She had flown from Kenya and she would be getting into the big plane that had been waiting on the apron. And that was much nearer to him. She would be a clearer target when she tried to board it.

There were still no guards outside the building, police or army. The small party had now reached the building and the people with her were standing aside as she entered. Now he must stay alert until she came out again.

He was getting stiff as he waited. Would she ever come? He had no way of measuring time.

The rain, when it started, was carried in from the direction of the Lake on a light breeze. He pulled himself into the side of the hut which gave him some shelter. It was nothing to worry about. Now he could see the activity in the airport building. The doors were opening. Large trolleys were being wheeled across the tarmac by two of the airport's attendants. The smell of food. No-one else was following. The rain was light and the trolleys reached the large plane. He watched as they loaded. He checked the rifle.

The wind blew harder. The rain was heavier, driving along the runway. He was cold and he started shivering. He must move to make himself warmer and take the stiffness out of his limbs but if he did he might be seen. If he didn't his shivering might affect his aim. He risked rubbing his legs and arms to bring the life back into them.

There was movement in the front of the building. He pressed himself back into the wall of the outbuilding and gently pulled the rifle close to him. She was coming. He could see her shaking hands with a tall Muzungu. Others were bowing to her. She turned and the door was opened for her. She started to walk out. Beside her was a man who walked with his hands behind his back.

And then the storm hit. Not the devil throwing spears this time; a wind coming straight off the Lake which hit him like a punch. The rain was a torrent. It felt as though he was standing under the falls on the Sipi River. The building kept some of the rain off him but he was still drenched. They had gone back into the building. Now he had to wait again. He was tired, hungry and very wet. Would he be able to shoot straight? The storm kept blowing. He could still see people clustered around the door. He knew that storms like this could last a long time and then stop as abruptly as they started. Patience. Wait. The rain continued to lash down, the wind off the lake as strong as ever. So

138

much time passing. So much time to worry whether he would succeed.

It stopped. He had sheltered the rifle with his body against the wall of the building and now he lifted it and worked the bolt to load it ready for firing. The door opened. She was coming. She led; the man with his hands behind his back was at her side. A small group of other Wazungu followed. He raised the rifle to his shoulder. Squeeze, the army men all said. Don't jerk on the trigger. Wait a little longer until she was closer. He sighted the weapon and …… squeezed.

The explosion burst the breech of the rifle. A flash and then Juba felt the searing pain in his right eye. He flung his hands up to his face. The wrecked rifle lay at his feet. The Queen kept walking. She neither slowed nor quickened her pace. The man alongside her walked more quickly. He raised his arm protectively. Those behind her had stopped and were looking around. The doors of the building had been thrown open and people were coming out. Ants running in circles.

Where Juba stood no lights penetrated the blackness. He flung himself over the fence wire and ran as fast as he could towards the Lake. He could feel blood dripping down his face. His eye was on fire and he couldn't focus his sight. It was instinct alone that kept him going. He ran. On and on. The length of the perimeter fence was in complete darkness. He reached the lake shore as the Argonaut airliner roared above him on its way to El Adem and then England.

TWENTY-FIVE

A Uganda Police sergeant found the rifle by the edge of the runway. Confusion soon turned into pandemonium. Could it be that an attempt had been made on the Queen's life? The Assistant Commissioner of Police representing the forces of security for this important event spent more energy on castigating the Special Branch Senior Superintendent for having no forewarning of this than doing anything to track down the perpetrator. All of which later made for good dinner party stories.

Police started to search the area but by torchlight there was little to see to give any clues about where the failed assassin has gone.

Juba stopped running and crouched down on the beach. If he could muster the energy and spirit to keep going he might reach the taxi park where Nyoka had said he would be. Now he knew how a buffalo hit by a drop spear might feel – intent on flight until it dropped dead. How far was it? He didn't know Entebbe well. It was a place of Wazungu and Wahindi, not Africans. But he was on the shore and the taxi park was near the lake. He moved his hand gingerly towards his eye. Even the slightest movement brought such pain that he thought he would faint. He daren't touch it. Move on. Find Nyoka.

He was in fact nearer to the taxi park than he realised. The only vehicle there was the black Peugeot. The door swung open and he heard the command from inside. 'Move yourself. Get in.' Nyoka leant across him and pulled the door to, driving away as he did so. The estate car sped past the Botanical Gardens and then veered off onto a track. When the car was sheltered by trees Nyoka stopped. Juba managed to splutter out the events that led him to the taxi. Nyoka struck a match and by its light looked at Juba's face. 'It's bad. We must get out of here fast. We'll go through the villages.' Juba groaned. How could he survive the ruts and holes of the minor roads? As if reading his mind Nyoka added, 'We can't go on the main road. There will be road blocks.'

Juba passed out as they bounced along the rutted tracks but Nyoka's local knowledge got them to Kampala without being stopped. He pulled up alongside a house that Juba didn't recognise. 'Stay in the car and keep your head down,' ordered the taxi man. Minutes later he was back with Fulani.

The Kenyan used a torch to look at Juba's face. He ignored the minor wounds where metal splinters had ripped into facial tissue, concentrating on the right eye. 'This needs proper attention.'

'What do you mean,' asked Juba.

'African medicine isn't going to do much for you.'

'But I can't go to the hospital …'

'You won't have to. Nyoka knows where we are going.'

The taxi weaved its way through the warren of streets of Old Kampala. The pain had taken its toll and Fulani and Nyoka had to manhandle Juba along a dark passageway. Fulani knocked on a door. A muffled voice asked in Swahili who was there. Juba couldn't hear Fulani's response but the door inched open and an Indian appeared. 'Quickly, bring him in here,' said the man. Juba was helped into a sparsely furnished, ill lit room. 'Sit down there,' and the man pointed to a chair. The Indian leant over Juba and with a strong flashlight examined his face. He turned to Fulani and in confidential tones started to say, 'There are metal splinters …'

Juba stopped him. 'They are my injuries. Tell me,

141

not him.'

The Indian looked at Fulani who nodded. 'What have you been doing? There are metal splinters in your eye. And there are some in other parts of your face though they aren't serious.' He continued to look closely at the eye, shaking his head. 'It is very bad. I will do what I can tonight. You will have to come back.' He left the room and when he came back he carried a white linen roll of surgical instruments. With tweezers he started to remove the steel shards from Juba's face, dropping them into an enamel dish. 'Now for the one in the eye.' He said this as though whispering to himself. Juba lost consciousness as he removed the large splinter. When he awoke he found himself in his own house, a large pad of lint covering his right eye. He could make out Fulani's face as he stood by his bed. 'So you didn't succeed. What happened?'

'It was going well until the rain came. When she came out I aimed and fired. I don't know what happened then. I thought someone had shot at me but if I had been hit in the eye by a bullet I would be dead. I think the rifle blew up in my face.'

'I suppose you did what you could. I have informed them in Kenya. They won't like it but I don't think they will blame you. We'll never have such a chance again.'

'You took me to a doctor ...'

'He is an Indian. You don't need to know any more than his family are all in Kenya and he is aware that we know where they live. He said you have got to go back to see him. He said your eye is bad.'

The Assistant Commissioner CID drove into the Old Fort on Nakasero Hill. He carried a parcel under his arm as he walked into the Quartermaster's Office. 'There you are George,' he said as he put the parcel on the desk and opened it. 'What do you make of that?'

George Bliss looked at the rifle and reached for a file on the shelf behind him. He looked quickly down a list and nodded. 'It's one of the broomstick brigade, though I guess you knew that.'

'Yes, I thought it was. You're the firearms expert; tell me what happened to it.'

Bliss picked up the shattered weapon and examined it. 'It was a blow-back. Looks to me as though the barrel was dirty inside and when it was discharged the round jammed. The person firing it would have got a face full.'

'So we should be checking the medical people for someone with facial injuries?'

'That's about the size of it.' Bliss sat holding the gun, shaking his head. 'It makes you think doesn't it … if someone had used a bit of oily flannelette four by two and a pull through before it was fired … I shudder to think of it. Is it public knowledge?'

'We've sat on it hard, George. As far as anyone knows it was just another quiet night at Entebbe.'

Following Fulani's instructions Juba remained in his house for several days. One evening Nyoka's taxi collected him and took him to Old Kampala. The doctor removed his eye.

TWENTY-SIX

Before they had left Mbale Rosemary had started to live her own life rather than being some sort of adjunct to Cecil. All this was due to Flora. She had watched her as she developed her craft with the pride that a mother reserves for her children. Although she would never say so to anyone else – particularly Cecil – she was proud, too, of the way she had learned a difficult local language and had worked out a system for the mute Flora to communicate with her. The sadness amid all this was she had no Father Con with whom to celebrate what she had achieved.

Now in Entebbe she was getting the same feelings of frustration again, asking herself the same questions. What was more, there was no view of Mount Elgon to console her in the early hours of the morning. She missed the mystery of the mountain which overshadowed the Township – the way its moods changed. True, there had been the novelty of being on a different station and meeting new people but this had worn off. Since the accession of the new Queen Cecil was working long hours. She saw so little of him that she yearned to be back on one of the up-country stations before he was promoted to District Commissioner. The move had not affected Flora's output. Her bank balance had extended too; not of course that she knew what a bank balance was, despite Rosemary's best efforts to inform her. She just knew that she had a lot of money.

Rosemary had returned to her early morning habit of rising before dawn and watching the sun. Instead of looking out over a dark mountain she now had the lake. The night had been stickily humid and before dawn she had taken the old steamer chair out onto the lawn at the back of the house. As she watched the first glimmer of light she was conscious of someone's presence. She turned to find Flora standing near the chair. 'You like watching the sun rise, too, Flora?' It was now light enough to see the signs Flora made.

'Yes. But not here. I want to go back to the place I know. Where there aren't any lake flies swarming, biting me.'

'I used to like watching Elgon wake up.'

Flora continued signing. 'Elgon. I want to go back to that place. It was where I was born.'

'Go back? You remember when the Deesee found you; they were going to kill you. Surely they would still try.'

'They wouldn't if Mrs Deesee was there with me.'

'You want me to go there with you? I'm afraid that is out of the question.'

'You are not happy here. You were different when we were in Mbale.'

'It wouldn't work. I'm no longer Mrs Deesee.'

'You still are to them.'

How can you argue with someone when they can only use sign language? Still, the old woman was striking some chords and it was clear she had more to tell her. 'What would you do if you went back?'

'I still have land there. I have a house on it if it hasn't been burnt. There's more land than I need and there is good water in the stream. You tell me I have a lot of money. Do I have enough to take down the old house and replace it with one built of stone blocks like a Mzungu house? With a corrugated iron roof?'

'I'm sure you have more than enough to do that.'

'Then I will build a house. It will have four rooms. One for me, one for cooking and eating and one for you.'

'You said four rooms…'

145

'Yes, three and a big one for me to make and sell my little people. Visitors will come to Elgon and we will make money for the local people. They won't kill me then, will they? I have thought about this a lot. I could not do it if you don't come and do what you do here. You have to come.' Rosemary wondered if she understood the signing correctly. Was Flora really suggesting she should go with her to Elgon? She started to go over it all again.

It was fully light now and she could hear Cecil moving in the house. He appeared on the verandah dressed ready for work. 'Rosemary, what on earth have you been doing out here all this time? You and Flora had your heads together so long I had breakfast. I'm off to work.'

Rosemary saw him turn to leave the house. 'Cecil, hold on a moment I've something to tell you.'

'I'm sure it can wait until I come back this evening.' With that he strode off.

That was the decisive moment. 'Flora. I am coming with you. We will make it work.' And have fun while we are doing it, she said to herself.

TWENTY-SEVEN

They arrived in Mbale in the late afternoon. Rosemary's small estate car was loaded with all the safari kit that had been packed away, forgotten, in the house in Entebbe – pressure lamps, primus stove, cooking utensils, water filter, and more. She had even remembered to buy a five gallon tin of kerosene at one of the Indian shops at Entebbe before they left.

Rosemary drove into the yard behind the District Police HQ. She removed her hat, shook the dust out of her hair and went in to see Tug Wilson. 'I'm surprised to see you back here. You might have let me know you were coming,' said the policeman.

'I didn't know myself until this morning. You remember Flora?' Tug Wilson looked puzzled but nodded. 'She owns a plot of land on Elgon. She says she had a house there if it hasn't been destroyed. She's got quite a fortune in the bank from her sculpting and she's going to use some of her money to build a new house.'

'I suppose you'll drop her off and go back to Entebbe.'

'No, Tug, she still needs some help from me. I'm staying until she has her business up and running.'

'How long is that going to take?'

'I really don't know. As long as it takes, I guess.'

'Rosemary for Heavens sake …. Have you gone out of your mind? You know all the trouble we have had on Elgon and that woman….'

'You mean Flora?'

'Yes, Flora.'

'Calm down Tug. It may seem strange to you but it isn't to me.'

'Cecil must be mad to let you do this.'

147

'Cecil won't approve when he hears but he'll just have to lump it.'

'Doesn't he know what you are doing?'

'Not yet, but he will. Around seven this evening. He didn't seem interested this morning so I've left him a note.'

'What on earth has happened to you Rosemary?' He was about to continue but when he saw the glint in Rosemary's eye he thought better of it.

'Nothing really, Tug, other than seeing some light. Any chance of a bed for the night?

'I was going to offer you one. I couldn't let you go this late in the day and if you are still set on doing this you can get an early start in the morning. As far as we know all the trouble has died down. My detectives never did find that man Wanyama. They are sure he was the one responsible for all the trouble on the mountain and at Magodes. The information they have got says that thanks to your identity parade he has left the district.'

Scatty Muller arrived at the Public Works Department compound in Kampala as the gates were being opened. He had ground his way through session after session with the physiotherapist in readiness for this morning. And now he sat in the Land Rover. If he could master driving with his artificial leg he would be allowed to take the vehicle back to his camp. He'd be working again on the job he loved. If he failed he didn't know what he would do. They'd hinted they would offer him a desk job. If they did he had already decided he'd turn it down.

When he had arrived he was confident that he would be able to drive again but now that he was sitting in the Land Rover his left leg, amputated below the knee, felt useless. He looked down at the clutch pedal. It was bigger than the clutch of a car and he knew it took more effort to move it. He guided his foot onto the pedal. He pushed. The pedal went half way down. He could move it no further. He tried again and again. Still he couldn't depress it to the floor. He climbed out of the vehicle and walked round the compound. Although it was only 8.30 he was sweating heavily. He climbed back into the cab and tried again. This time it went down further. He started the engine, pushed as hard as he could and moved the gear stick. It was more than an hour before he could manage the vehicle to his own satisfaction. With his shirt wet with perspiration he went to the office.

'Can't let you go until I've tested you,' said the Transport Officer. Two hours later Scatty was collecting his belongings and was on his way.

In Mbale he was greeted by Charles Harkness. 'Am I glad to see you? Your gang are still up at the camp. They've kept it in good order. Your truck is there too.' He spent two days making arrangements for stores and materials and as soon as he could escape the well wishers he made his way up *his* road.

He drove into the compound. All the gangers were lined up like a military parade. The Headman, Petero Odoi, stood proudly in front of the rank and as Scatty climbed down from the Land Rover Odoi swung the Mannlicher rifle up into a salute. The torch was still tied to the barrel. 'Where the hell did you get that, I thought it was lost for ever.'

'I found it near the cave of elephants and hid it until you came back.'

'They tell me the trouble has all died down. Has it?'

'There has been no trouble since the shooting of the Mzungu policeman. They say it is quiet because General Elgon has gone away. He was the one who made the trouble. He led the attack on our camp.'

'So he was responsible for me losing my leg. He's got a lot to answer for. I can't remember seeing him, but if I do meet up with him …' Scatty didn't finish the sentence but Odoi saw he was patting the rifle. 'I'll feel a lot safer now I've got "Old Trusty" back.'

Scatty toured the camp starting with his rondavel. It was spotless – no trace of Simba's blood now. The biggest surprise was the equipment. He found Bansilal, Harkness's mechanic, putting the finishing touches to painting the plant he had repaired. Bright yellow with black lettering. With a flourish the Indian gave it one last stroke with the paint brush and wiped his hands down his overalls. 'There you are Mr. Muller. Like new isn't it?'

'If it works as well as it looks I'll be very happy.' To his delight he found that Bansilal had also repaired the holes in the fuel tank of his truck. He sent for the Headman. 'Petero, tomorrow to celebrate being back I'm going to give the biggest braai you've ever seen. I want people around here to come and enjoy it too. And it might make sure we have them with us in future rather than being against us.'

The sun was just rising when the two of them set off down the winding road to the plain in Scatty's truck. They drove until they spotted the herd of Uganda Kob grazing on the dewy grass. It took Scatty just three shots to bring down two of the largest. 'I'm back. I'm living, even if I've only got one good leg,' he yelled in joy. Between them they hauled the carcases onto the back of the truck and the engine laboured under the load as they returned to the camp.

The fire was lit early, the buck were prepared and the long starting processes of the braai began. By dusk the tempting smell of roasting meat was carried across into the village by the breeze and gradually the local people were drawn to the camp. Scatty had found his old bamboo chair and planted it comfortably close to the fire. The singing started, that wonderful sound that comes from African voices in unison. There was no other sound like it, he thought. Gourds of maize beer were passed around. And then the dancing, the drumming ... it should have been a joy to his ears but suddenly he was back in the horror of that last braai. He was startled by a touch on his shoulder. *They had got that close without him seeing them. It was all going to start again.* He shuddered and groped for "Old Trusty".

'You don't need that Scatty.' A woman's voice. A voice he would know anywhere after those days in the isolation ward. He stumbled as he tried to stand up. That bloody leg, or what's left of it. 'Rosemary. What are you doing here? I thought you were in Entebbe.'

'We've got some catching up to do, Scatty.' She sat down on the grass alongside his chair and told him her story. She ended with, 'You see, I'm your new neighbour on Elgon.'

TWENTY-EIGHT

There was no mistaking the Chevrolet sedan. It rolled like a ship in a storm as it took the rutted tracks but it sailed along them with ease. Rosemary stood at the door and watched its progress as it climbed the last hundred yards towards Flora's house. The familiar figure climbed out of the vehicle, waiting a moment, holding the car door open as though uncertain whether to stay or get back into the car and drive off. At last he pushed the door to and started to climb the steps to the house. She stood at the door wondering what her husband would say. He wasn't dressed in the Entebbe uniform of well pressed shorts and crisp white shirt. He had reverted to bush jacket.

'It took me the devil of a time to find this house,' were his opening words. 'It wasn't here last time I came.'

'This is a surprise Cecil.'

'I made my mind up ...'

'You must have been up early to get here at this hour.' She had been dreading this moment. She knew he had to come sooner or later but funnily enough standing here at Flora's threshold she was feeling composed.

'Well before it was light. I wanted to make sure we had plenty of time to talk.'

'That's fine but you've had a long journey. I was just about to have breakfast. How about you?' He nodded. 'No Kellogg's from South Africa, I'm afraid. Fresh paw paw and avocados picked from our own trees, roast yams and coffee from our bushes. We'll have it out here on the verandah. You can admire the view while I get the food ready.'

Woolly Bill sat and looked out over the lower

slopes. The air was cool and fresh. Rosemary. She was different. More content than he had seen her in a long time. And was that because he hadn't *really* seen her for a long time? For once in his married life he felt at a loss for what to say and how to say it. He sat alone with these thoughts until she reappeared carrying a tray with the food. She sat and poured the coffee. They ate in silence for some minutes before both started to talk at the same time. 'Go on, Cecil, ... I'll listen.'

'Well, you may have wondered why it has taken me a month to come ...'

'No, not really.'

'I won't plead that I have been swamped with work, though that's a fact.'

'You always have been since you got to Entebbe.'

'I thought by now you might have realised you'd made a mistake in coming ....'

'Really? What makes you think I have made a mistake? ...'

'Well, I knew I'd have to give it long enough for you to find out, then it dawned on me that you were at your happiest, in the early days, when you came on safari with me. I thought being up here with Flora is your way of recreating that. I ought to come ...'

'You know, you're the same old Cecil. You're not really listening to a word I'm saying. You're way off beam. You'll be telling me soon that I'm having a mid-life crisis. Well, perhaps I am. The truth is I was fed up with not being me, just being Mrs. Deesee – that's what the Africans called me and it was picked up by some of the Europeans too, though I doubt if you heard it. Being good at entertaining, supervising the cook making a curry lunch for Heaven knows how many, chairing all those meetings which was only about keeping people sweet. "Oh that Mrs. Deesee is so charming ..."

'You're exaggerating ...'

'No I'm not. It took Flora to show me what I was capable of. You haven't even asked after her or seen her yet. Come inside.' Together they went into the house. Flora was in her room polishing one of the many statuettes and busts that stood on her work bench. 'Look at those. A party of American tourists is coming next week and she will sell all of them and more if she could make them. You'd never believe the money she made while we were in Entebbe. It was Flora that had this house built. I had no money to contribute. We're a partnership; her craftsmanship and my business management. The next item on the agenda is building a visitor centre and that will make money for the local people.'

'I had no idea ...'

'It wasn't like that once but that's the way it is now, Cecil.'

He looked up into space, trying to recall. 'You remember that early morning in Mbale when I wanted a penny for your thoughts? I think I should have found those extra pennies.' She nodded; yes she remembered, it was when all this started. 'Would you have told me?'

'I wouldn't have known how to then.'

So where does that leave us now?'

'Me here and you in Entebbe.'

'We can't leave it like this, Rosemary ...'

'Why not? For the first time in years I'm enjoying being who I am.'

'Look, this has made me do some thinking. Because of all the war years without long leave I qualify soon for early retirement, if I want to take it. The pension will be good. I was thinking we could settle somewhere in the West Country in England. There would be plenty for you to do there.'

'Wet cold austerity England. Food, clothes and petrol rationing. No thanks. I'm not ready for that yet.'

They returned to the breakfast table on the verandah and finished the coffee. Cecil looked defeated. He stood up and moved to the top of the steps. 'I don't know what else to say. I might as well go back then. I've nothing more to offer.'

'Cecil, you've lost the habit of considering me as a person – you used to when we first came out. Maybe you'll think about that in the odd moments you have as you draft the constitution. At least now we've met and you know how I am. I realise your work in Entebbe is important. Get that done and then … who knows?' She reached up and kissed him on the cheek. She watched the Chevrolet bump its way down the hill until it was out of sight.

Scatty threw himself into his road building. Bansilal had done a good job. He had replaced the broken parts, tuned the motors of the rollers, the grader and dumper truck and now the road making plant was better than before the raid on his camp. He worked long hours letting nothing distract him. Each night when he came back to his rondavel he felt compelled to look up at the lamp hook. He could still see Simba hanging there. At first he broke down sobbing. With time he overcame his grief. But not his anger.

His hand brushed the artificial leg and this made him think of his time in hospital, the flight to Kampala and, of course, Rosemary. He hadn't seen her since the night of the braai. He wondered how was she coping living up here without the amenities that she had in Mbale. It seemed to him a strange choice to be staying with that African woman who was a mute. No good just wondering; he ought to pay her a visit.

He drove his truck the short distance to where Odoi said the house had been built. There on the side of a hill stood a building of concrete blocks with a red painted corrugated iron roof. The outside had been whitewashed and shone in the pure light of morning. A veranda ran the length of the house. Above the front door was a large painted sign, FLORA. At the side and around the back of the house grew a variety of crops. Cooking bananas which from their abundance had been there for a long time, tomato plants beginning to mature, maize poking shoots through the rich soil, sorghum. Almost any plant grew fast in this climate. A thatched granary stood some thirty feet from the back of the house.

The sound of the motor brought Rosemary to the door. She waved as she saw Scatty climbing down from the Land Rover. 'At last you've come to see our house. Come in and have some coffee. I was just making some.'

He climbed the steep flight of steps leading up to the house. 'My word, it looks pretty good, but aren't you going to miss living in a Township like Mbale? With all the mod cons – electricity, proper sanitation, piped water for a start.'

'You forget, Scatty, I've lived up-country in some pretty raw places. When Cecil and I first came out from England he did all his safaris by bicycle and porters carrying the camping gear on their heads. I used to go with him. Come on, I'll show you round.' He was impressed with Flora's work room. She was busy mixing clay when he entered. She carried on working but acknowledged him with a smile. Her kiln stood in the corner of the room and there were several busts waiting for firing.

Being used to aluminium rondavels as up-country accommodation Scatty was amazed at the facilities. Rosemary saw his expression. 'You see we're not as basic as you thought. We've even got a generator for electric light. The people in the village are in awe.'

156

'I take back what I said. It must have cost you a packet.'

'It's Flora's place. It all comes from her work. She has done well with her sculptures. She said that if I was going to live here with her it had to be done properly. It had never hit me until then that I was dependent on Cecil for everything. I had no income of my own. Some how or other I had to start making my own way.'

He felt embarrassed by Rosemary disclosing this. He switched the subject. 'Whoever built the house did a good job'

'One of the PWD men from Mbale was going to do it – moonlighting I suppose - but when I saw all the cement and blocks were from the PWD stores I made him take them back. I don't think Cecil would be happy if Tug arrested Flora while I was her house guest. I got in touch with Joginder Singh, the builder in Mbale, and he built in it in no time at all.'

'We've been through a lot, you and I. Elgon hasn't been the luckiest of places for either of us. Do you really feel safe here now after all that?

'Yes I do. At first I thought the local people were going to carry on their feud with Flora but once I told them what she wanted to do – get tourists in to buy her sculptures bringing them work and money – things changed. She had to promise that there wouldn't be any likenesses of any people from the village though. It helps that I speak their language, thanks to dear old Father Con. I think his spirit is pretty close.' She sighed, 'I don't think I'll ever want to leave this place.'

'Don't ever want to leave? What about Woolly ... sorry, I mean Cecil? I'd assumed you were only going to stay here until Flora was fully up and running and then go back to Entebbe.'

'Cecil has been here to see me. I have to admit he's not very pleased but I'm sure it's more to do with what my staying here will do to his image. Cecil never shows his feelings or talks about them.'

'I'll still worry about you. Don't get lulled into a false sense of security. It only wants someone like that guy who called himself General Elgon to appear and things could change very quickly.'

'Don't worry, Scatty. I'm sure we're safe now. The word is that he has gone away. For good.'

Juba Wanyama fretted. He hated the cramped living conditions in the over-populated Katwe village. It was nothing more than an unpleasant sprawling suburb of Kampala. He was cooped up in his house during daylight hours in case any of the swarm of police informers talked of a man who had lost his eye. After the failure at Entebbe the police must be looking for such a person. He was taking no exercise and his physical condition was suffering because of it. He had to do something; he had taken to going out to nearby bars. He wore dark glasses even though he only went at night-time. He drank too much – often the freshly distilled spirit which the locals called waragi, rough and raw brought in from the stills in the swamps on the backs of bicycles, still warm. This was no good, it was stupid. He could take no more of this existence. The life of a hyena, hiding up by day and creeping out at night to scavenge what he could.

Fulani came on one of his infrequent visits. He could smell the odour of stale drink which permeated the atmosphere of the house. 'It's time you moved on, Juba. Sooner or later you'll be picked up by the polisi. There's nothing more you can do for us here. You must go to Kenya. You will be yourself again when you are in the forests. Get the train tomorrow.'

The following day Juba bundled his few possessions into his bedding roll and took a pirate taxi to Kampala railway station. He had no intention of going straight through to Kenya. There was still something he had to do in Uganda.

TWENTY-NINE

The journey to Tororo dragged. At times the train travelled so slowly that he could have got down and walked alongside it. At Tororo he had to change for Mbale. It was dark before he reached the end of Scatty's new road.

He took it for granted that there would be local people who would be pleased to earn a reward from the polisi if they knew he was back. He made his way to the caves he used when he was General Elgon. He would sleep there then settle his business tomorrow. He had to find that old woman. She had much to answer for. The picture Fulani's tame policeman had shown him before he went to Kampala had deeply affected him. It was as though she had looked right into his soul when she made the statuette that had been photographed. But how could she do that? Yes, he had lived on Elgon when he was a child but he had been taken to Kenya by his father when he was very young. Even if she had seen him then how could she know enough about him to make such an image?

The following day he waited until it was nearly dusk and then roamed the area looking for her house. He thought he knew where to find it. It should have been close to where the chief had burned, but all he could see standing where her house should have been was a bright new building – more Muzungu style than African. This was going to be more difficult than he had at first thought. Who would build a new house like that? It couldn't be the old woman; she would never do that. She must have sold the land. That would mean she had probably left the area. He went back to the cave. He had brought cooked maize meal with him and he ate this cold not wanting wood smoke to attract anyone.

He woke late. Towards the evening he ventured out. It was still light and he wore his large straw hat. With the beard he had grown in Katwe and dark glasses he felt safe. To add to the disguise he affected a slight limp, reducing his height by hunching his back. He tested this by going to one of the small bars and buying banana beer. It was the end of the week, the bar was crowded and he could see some of the road making gang all laughing together in one corner. None of them looked his way. These people all came from around Tororo - in Buganda they called the people from that area "the Naked Ones" to show their contempt for their ignorance.

No-one was taking any notice of him. Give it a little longer and he could try to seek out the old woman again. He didn't enjoy the beer but he finished it slowly. To leave any would raise suspicion – who would pay for beer and then not drink it all?

Scatty was in his compound sitting by the fire. He loved the crackling of the dried twigs as they burned and he threw another handful into the flames. Saturday. Work over for the week. Petero and boys off on the booze. And why not, they'd earned it. They'd worked hard enough all week. He turned the skewer of meat over the flames and then settled down to cleaning "Old Trusty", even though it didn't need it. He removed the bolt and looked down the inside of the barrel, the firelight reflecting along the unblemished shiny surface. Before it happened he would have been throwing snippets of meat to Simba who would be toasting his paws alongside him. *But it did happen.* He could scream it out. *It ... did ... happen.* And nothing would ever be the same again. And now there was Rosemary as a neighbour. How they had talked when they were in the isolation ward together. He turned the meat again.

What it must be to have someone like her to share your life with. Nonsense thinking about it, though. She was Woolly Bill's wife for Heavens sake. Why was life so complicated? He was lost in his thoughts when the Headman called his name. 'Mr. Scatty. I have seen him.' Petero had run all the way from the village and was panting. 'I have seen him. What will you do?'

'Slow down Petero. Get your breath back and tell me who you have seen.'

'The man calling himself "General Elgon"

'That man. Where?'

'In the bar.'

'Are you sure it was him.'

'I know it was him. I saw enough of him when we had the trouble. He is trying to make himself look different. He has grown a beard and wears dark glasses.'

'Did he know you saw him?'

'No. I'm sure he didn't.' The Headman was hopping from one leg to the other. 'Come on Mr. Scatty, we may not get the chance again … your leg … Simba. Hurry … are you going to kill him?'

Scatty got up from his place by the fire. He replaced the bolt in his rifle and loaded the magazine from ammunition in his pocket. 'Yes, if it's really him. Come on. You can show him to me.' He started to go towards his truck.

'No Mr. Scatty. We go by foot. The sound of the truck will scare him off.'

Rosemary had been down to Mbale Township for supplies. While she was there she collected her mail from her Post office box. There was a letter confirming that the party of American tourists were actually coming in a few days. She was excited at the thought. A first – her promotional efforts were going to pay off.

She hurried back to give Flora the good news. It was still light when she parked her old estate car by the house. It was good to be back in the cool mountain air after the humidity of the township. Flora was removing some of her work from the kiln as she walked in. 'They're good. You get better all the time, Flora. I don't know how you do it.' The African woman beamed and when Rosemary gave her the news she came from the kiln to hug her. We're going to need all of those and more when the Americans come.' *If only she could speak.*

Juba went from the bar to where the old woman's house had stood. Even though he was seventy yards or so from the house it was still light enough for him to see someone moving around. He stood by a bamboo grove and watched. Light flooded out through the windows and open door. He heard the throbbing of a generator. Shadows moving around. Someone inside the house. Was it the old woman? Then he saw the rear doors of the estate car parked at the side of the house. He knew that car. He had been in it. Mrs. Deesee. What was she doing here? The old woman had lived at the back of the DC's house in Mbale. Mrs. Deesee must know where she was. He started to move towards the house.

A premonition? There wasn't any particular noise that made her go to the door. A man wearing a straw hat was climbing the steps towards the house. A beard covered much of his face. There was something strangely familiar about him. In the local language she asked 'Can I help you?'

'I can speak English.' That voice. She had no doubt who it was. Her mind was back digging clay when this man stood at the top of the pit and a string of nightmares began.

Scatty and his Headman pushed on along the track which led through mango trees to the village. As they came to the edge of the thicket Odoi swung his arm up across Scatty's chest and put his finger to his lips. A hundred yards away was Flora's house and a man was climbing up towards it. 'It's him,' he whispered. He pointed to the path that would take them close without being seen. As they loped along the track Scatty could see Rosemary at the door. She stood one arm across the entrance barring the man's way. He could just hear what he said.

'I want to see the old woman.'

Rosemary stiffened. 'Why should I let you? You have caused enough trouble already.'

'I do not want to harm you but I will if you don't let me see her. She must tell me something.' He pulled a long knife from his belt. In trying to peer into the house to see Flora he didn't hear Scatty. He turned to face him when the rifle was pushed into his back. Scatty moved fast. The gun smashed down on his hand and the knife fell. Odoi pounced on it shouting, 'Shoot him Mr. Scatty.'

'If you are going to shoot me then do it. But first I have something I must know from the old woman.'

Scatty kept his finger on the trigger but Juba's request puzzled him. 'What do you want from her?'

'I want to ask her about something important to me. I want to look in her face when I ask her.'

Rosemary stood back from the doorway and looked at Scatty. She could see his raised eyebrows but he nodded and she motioned Juba to enter. Flora was sat at her workbench, her hands clasped in her lap. She was looking directly at Juba. Rosemary spoke in the old woman's tongue. When Flora had finished signing Rosemary said, 'She will answer any question you ask.'

Scatty was bewildered. Why humour the damned man? He didn't deserve it. But if that was what Rosemary wanted. He prodded him forward with his rifle.

Juba stumbled forward towards Flora. Rosemary thought how different he looked from when she first saw him at the clay pit. This was no longer the tall, muscular athlete with the arrogant air, whose appearance intimidated her. This man with the reputation of a ruthless killer now seemed to be pleading as he spoke to Flora in her own language. Rosemary translated for Scatty, 'He says he wants to know how Flora could make a statuette of him that turned him inside out – no-one could do that. That's the best I can make of what he is saying.'

The old woman turned slowly to the rack of statuettes on the bench and selected one which she pulled forward. It was the image of Juba, the one that had stood in the identity parade. Rosemary doubted that she would be able to interpret the complexities that must be coming next. To her amazement the words came slowly from Flora's own lips. A beautifully toned soft voice. Juba seemed to grow smaller, his head bowed.

Rosemary translated. 'I think I've got it right. "*A mother never loses the ability to reach right inside her son.*"' As she said this Flora swung round and gripped the pestle from her mixing bowl and smashed it down on the statuette. It crumpled into pieces. She slammed the implement into the remains and ground them into dust and spoke again.

Rosemary was at a loss for words then she managed, 'She said "*a long time ago I had a son but he left me. I have waited. Hoping. But I have no hope. I have no son.*"'

Flora spoke again. Rosemary translated. '*She is*

165

saying kill him if you wish, send him away if you wish. I don't care what happens to him.'

Scatty prodded Juba with his rifle. It was as though he had red mist behind his eyes. Simba, poor headless bloody Simba. 'You. Outside,' and he drove Juba out of the house at rifle point.

He stopped as they turned towards the side of the house and brought the rifle up to his shoulder. 'Turn round and face me.' Juba turned. Scatty aimed. And then he lowered the rifle. 'Voetsek. This is just what my bloody old man would have done. Shoot you. Pull the trigger, that's what he would have done without even thinking about it. Oh, man, how you deserve it but I won't let you make me be like him. Clear off. Get off this mountain. I never want to see you again.'

'Mr. Scatty, what are you doing? You know how bad he is. He tried to kill you, he tried to kill Mrs. Deesee. He killed Father Con. And what about Simba? He shouldn't live.'

'Sorry if I disappoint you Petero. ' He emptied "Old Trusty's" magazine and put the bullets in the pocket of his bush jacket. The Headman wandered off shaking his head, clicking his tongue. Juba Wanyama walked away down the hill. Scatty could see him no more in the darkness of the evening. He turned and went back into the house to Rosemary.

EPILOGUE

1954

Major Dick Browning, the Army liaison officer for the Aberdare Forest area near Mount Kenya, stood in the clearing. The forest with its tall hardwoods loomed over everything like a monstrous tidal wave, waiting to swamp the clearing and the village. There were the British army, Kenya Police, Kings African Rifles, Kenya Regiment – enlisted from the European population – and hardest bedfellow of the lot, the Home Guard, local Africans led by local Europeans who often disappeared into the jungle with no means of contact. Holding together their activities was a job loaded with impossibilities.

He had been forewarned of what was coming. He glanced again at the trail emerging from deep in the forest and then looked at the second lieutenant standing next to him. He eyed the smooth face that looked as though it had no need of a razor, the tight lips and the white knuckles gripping the Patchett machine carbine.

How many times in his military life had he been here. At nineteen, the living skeletons of Belsen - and the dead ones too. At twenty-two the King David Hotel in Palestine, unleashing the kind of terrorism he realised even then would grind away at civilisation for ever more. Unstoppable. As if that wasn't enough, a posting to Cyprus and the bloody brutality of EOKA. Shots in the dark, neighbour on neighbour, cousin on cousin. These memories continually hammered Browning's heart. Now second lieutenant Michael Pymm, lately of Sandhurst and Preston Barracks in Lancashire, would get his first dose of red-blooded soldiering. He could at least give the young officer some respite.

'Soon there'll be things you don't need to see, Mike. Make your way back to the Land Rover.'

'Sir, is that necessary?'

'Yes it is and I'll tell you why. Come next year, or the year after, twenty years time even, whenever, there'll be an enquiry. Some politico will want to cover his arse, or some other politico will be looking for a quid pro quo or to curry favour or stick one up the other lot. All in the name of statesmanship. What you don't see you won't be able to testify to.'

'Sir, will that really happen …'

'I'd bet my life on it. No more questions. Just do as I say and take those squaddies with you.' He pointed to the infantrymen who had accompanied them.

'Sir. It's the KAR coming, isn't it?' The young officer saluted and turned away.

By now a crowd of local people had gathered. Out of the forest edge came a platoon of African soldiers headed by a tall sergeant, the heavyweight bulk of his body straining to burst out of the sweat sodden woollen khaki shirt. He strutted as if he were on the Queen's Birthday parade. Immediately behind him marched two private soldiers, shoulder to shoulder, holding their rifles high above their heads like jubilant standard bearers but instead of flags they each had a fixed bayonet. On each bayonet was a human head. The clearing echoed to the voices of the platoon singing the marching song of the KAR. There was a rumbling in the crowd. The women's' high pitched ululating wail broke out. Browning noticed most of the men were looking at the ground and not at the spectacle before them.

The crowd now was even thicker and the parading soldiers seemed oblivious to the British officer.

Browning raised his voice to be heard among the noise. Twice he yelled out, 'Sergeant'. The N.C.O. looked around, saw the officer and called his men to a halt. He marched across to Browning pushing anyone blocking him out of the way. He stopped eye to eye with the major and as he stamped his foot down his arm swung up to salute with military precision. 'Number One platoon, C Company 4th Battalion Kings African Rifles Uganda, Sir.'

The dreadlocks on the impaled heads were matted and their faces caked with mud. There were open wounds on the face of one head but the other head bore no marks. On this head one eye was open, staring straight ahead. There was no other eye just skin stretched over the empty socket, testimony to an injury gained long ago. No flies had settled on it. Browning felt as though he was looking at the works of an African sculptor. 'Remove them from the bayonets, Sergeant. I'll take some photographs for the records and then you will see they get a proper burial according to the customs of their tribe.' The sergeant's look said that Browning's head should take the place of one on a bayonet.

'Do you know who they are?'

The Sergeant pointed to one. 'They called him Fulani. He wasn't important.' He pointed to the other head. 'It was not difficult to find out the name of this one, Sir. He was important this one. He was known to everyone. He was General Elgon.'

Sources of Information

I have planted my fiction in a bed of fact. I can personally vouch for one of the key historical events; I was at Entebbe airport on the night the new Queen Elizabeth flew out to England. Even today I shiver as I feel that storm sweeping in from Lake Victoria. Other background came from a range of sources.

I refreshed my memories of the daily life of pre-Independent Uganda with Andrew Stuart's book "Of Cargoes, Colonies and Kings" (published by Radcliffe Press 2001). Andrew was a District Officer, and as the son of a missionary he knew African people from villagers to politicians to kings.

"Looking Back At The Uganda Protectorate" is a book rich in information about the work of District Officers. Douglas Brown persuaded nearly a hundred of his former colleagues to contribute to this. I know of no other source which gives such a sparkling account of the work and experiences of members of the Colonial Service. He published this in 1996 and I doubt if it ever got the circulation it deserved. One more volume captures this period of history well – "You Have Been Allocated Uganda" by Alan Forward (published by Poynington Publishing Company Dorset 1999), also a former District officer.

I know this underlines my technophobia but I still marvel at the information that can be gleaned electronically – for example about King George VI's illnesses and death; about Princess Elizabeth and the Duke of Edinburgh at Treetops Hotel and Sangana Lodge.

I found all of these sources valuable but I have to declare that any views expressed in the story are my own as are any errors.

Lightning Source UK Ltd.
Milton Keynes UK
UKOW02f0237280516

275152UK00003B/130/P